ESSENTIAL
BUKOWSKI

Essential Bukowski

poetry

Charles Bukowski

Selected and edited by
Abel Debritto

ecco

An Imprint of HarperCollinsPublishers

HarperCollins books may be purchased for educational, business, or sales promotional use. For information, please e-mail the Special Markets Department at SPsales@harpercollins.com.

A hardcover edition of this book was published in 2016 by Ecco, an imprint of HarperCollins Publishers.

FIRST ECCO PAPERBACK EDITION PUBLISHED 2018.

Designed by Suet Yee Chong

Library of Congress Cataloging-in-Publication Data has been applied for.

ISBN 978-0-06-256532-7

24 25 26 27 28 LBC 16 15 14 13 12

INTRODUCTION

With more than twenty Charles Bukowski poetry books now available in print and dozens of first-rate unpublished poems on file, an *essential* collection has been long overdue. The task at hand was titanic: A prolific author by any measure, with some five thousand poems on record written over a span of fifty years, Bukowski famously wrote almost every night in an alcoholic stupor, trashing most of the gibberish the morning after. Picking Bukowski's best poems out of this massive heap was daunting, to say the least.

"The bluebird," "the genius of the crowd," "roll the dice," "the crunch," and other popular poems were strong contenders even before I put together a tentative list. As I pored over both the published and the unpublished work, some relatively obscure gems, such as "when Hugo Wolf went mad," "sparks," "the loser," and "another academy" came back to life for me. I also included poems that were pivotal in Bukowski's career, like "swastika star buttoned to my ass," which moved longtime German translator, agent, and friend Carl Weissner to become a fervent Bukowski enthusiast after reading it in a small press magazine in England in 1966. There were one hundred and seventy poems in my final selection for the book, which then had to be cut down to only ninety-five—"democracy," "they, all of them, know," "the word," and other top-notch poems had to be discarded.

These ninety-five essential poems barely represent two percent of Bukowski's mammoth output, but his poetic evolution is hard to miss in this chronological collection. The early poems, with their lyricism and occasional surreal imagery, give way in the 1970s to Bukowski's "Dirty Old Man" macho persona, when he finally achieves success in his fifties, after which he takes, in his final years, a more philosophical stance on life. Through it all, what remains the same is Bukowski's brilliance at capturing things as they are, his crystal-clear snapshots of his immediate experiences as well as the world at large, which he hardly ever photoshopped after the fact.

It is precisely this genuineness, along with the timeless quality of Bukowski's most accomplished poems, that makes us embrace his poetry with open arms: the day-to-day but crucial trivialities found in "the shoelace"; the sensuality of "the shower"; the forces of life at work in "the mockingbird"; the tenderness of "love poem to Marina" and "the history of a tough motherfucker"; the elusive nature of art in many of the poems; the self-deprecating humor in "we've got to communicate"; the imperfection that makes us almost perfect in "one for the shoeshine man"; and the heartfelt portraits of the artists that Bukowski looks up to.

There's also the striking, disarming simplicity of "art" and "nirvana"; the Hemingwayesque spare lines of "Carson McCullers" and "hell is a lonely place"; the hymns to individualism and willpower of "no leaders" and "the genius of the crowd"; the never-take-things-for-granted spirit of "I met a genius"; the long narrative poems that read as well-paced short-stories; and the life-affirming drive of "the laughing heart" and "the crunch." These last two poems show that, despite the darkness that often entered his life and poetry, Bukowski always saw the light at the end of the tunnel, and we can't help but identify with that feeling.

These poems are Bukowski at his most captivating: unvarnished, witty, and passionate, showing us all "the way" as he listens to classical music on "a radio with guts" and drinks "the blood of the gods" in his small Los Angeles apartments and studios. The Buddha of San Pedro, Bukowski ultimately smiles because he knows the secret of it all is way beyond him, and that's the beauty of it: Bukowski distills life to its very essence, squeezing the magic out of the ordinary with his unmistakable, surpassing simplicity.

Essential, indeed.

friendly advice to a lot of young men,
and a lot of old men, too

Go to Tibet.
Ride a camel.
Read the Bible.
Paint your shoes blue.
Grow a beard.
Circle the world in a paper canoe.
Subscribe to the *Saturday Evening Post*.
Chew on the left side of your mouth only.
Marry a woman with one leg and shave with a straight razor.
And carve your name in her anus.

Brush your teeth with gasoline.
Sleep all day and climb trees at night.
Be a monk and drink buckshot and beer.
Hold your head under water and play the violin.
Do a belly dance before pink candles.
Kill your dog.
Run for mayor.
Live in a barrel.
Break your head with a hatchet.
Plant tulips in the rain.

But don't write any more poetry.

as the sparrow

To give life you must take life,
and as our grief falls flat and hollow
upon the billion-blooded sea
I pass upon serious inward-breaking shoals rimmed
with white-legged, white-bellied rotting creatures
lengthily dead and rioting against surrounding scenes.
Dear child, I only did to you what the sparrow
did to you; I am old when it is fashionable to be
young; I cry when it is fashionable to laugh.
I hated you when it would have taken less courage
to love.

layover

Making love in the sun, in the morning sun
in a hotel room
above the alley
where poor men poke for bottles;
making love in the sun
making love by a carpet redder than our blood,
making love while the boys sell headlines
and Cadillacs,
making love by a photograph of Paris
and an open pack of Chesterfields,
making love while other men—poor
fools—
work.

That moment—to this . . .
may be years in the way they measure,
but it's only one sentence back in my mind—
there are so many days
when living stops and pulls up and sits
and waits like a train on the rails.
I pass the hotel at 8
and at 5; there are cats in the alleys
and bottles and bums,
and I look up at the window and think,
I no longer know where you are,
and I walk on and wonder where
the living goes
when it stops.

the life of Borodin

the next time you listen to Borodin
remember he was just a chemist
who wrote music to relax;
his house was jammed with people:
students, artists, drunkards, bums,
and he never knew how to say "no."
the next time you listen to Borodin
remember his wife used his compositions
to line the cat boxes with
or to cover jars of sour milk;
she had asthma and insomnia
and fed him soft-boiled eggs
and when he wanted to cover his head
to hide out the sounds of the house
she only allowed him to use the sheet;
besides there was usually somebody
in his bed
(they slept separately when they slept
at all)
and since all the chairs
were usually taken
he often slept on the stairway
wrapped in an old shawl;
she told him when to cut his nails,
not to sing or whistle
or put too much lemon in his tea
or press it with a spoon;
Symphony #2 in B Minor
Prince Igor

In the Steppes of Central Asia
he could sleep only by putting a piece
of dark cloth over his eyes;
in 1887 he attended a dance
at the Medical Academy
dressed in a merrymaking national costume;
at last, he seemed exceptionally gay
and when he fell to the floor,
they thought he was clowning.

the next time you listen to Borodin,
remember . . .

when Hugo Wolf went mad

Hugo Wolf went mad while eating an onion
and writing his 253rd song; it was rainy
April and the worms came out of the ground
humming Tannhäuser, and he spilled his milk
with his ink, and his blood fell out to the walls
and he howled and he roared and he screamed, and
down-
stairs his landlady said, I *knew* it, that rotten son
of a
bitch has dummied up his brain, he's jacked-off
his last piece
of music and now I'll never get the rent, and some-
day he'll be famous
and they'll bury him in the rain, but right now
I wish he'd shut
up that god damned screaming—for my money he's
a silly pansy jackass
and when they move him out of here, I hope they
move in a good solid fisherman
or a hangman
or a seller of
biblical tracts.

destroying beauty

a rose
red sunlight;
I take it apart
in the garage
like a puzzle:
the petals are as greasy
as old bacon
and fall
like the maidens of the world
backs to floor
and I look up
at the old calendar
hung from a nail
and touch
my wrinkled face
and smile
because
the secret
is beyond me.

the day I kicked a bankroll out the window

and, I said, you can take your rich aunts and uncles
and grandfathers and fathers
and all their lousy oil
and their seven lakes
and their wild turkey
and buffalo
and the whole state of Texas,
meaning, your crow-blasts
and your Saturday night boardwalks,
and your 2-bit
library
and your crooked councilmen
and your pansy artists—
you can take all these
and your weekly newspaper
and your famous tornadoes
and your filthy floods
and all your yowling cats
and your subscription to *Life,*
and shove them, baby,
shove them.

I can handle a pick and ax again (I think)
and I can pick up
25 bucks for a 4-rounder (maybe);
sure, I'm 38
but a little dye can pinch the gray
out of my hair;
and I can still write a poem (sometimes),
don't forget *that,* and even if

they don't pay off,
it's better than waiting for death and oil,
and shooting wild turkey,
and waiting for the world
to begin.

all right, bum, she said,
get out.

what? I said.

get out. you've thrown your
last tantrum.
I'm tired of your damned tantrums:
you're always acting like a
character in an O'Neill play.

but I'm different, baby,
I can't help
it.

you're different, all right!
God, how different!
don't slam
the door
when you leave.

but, baby, I *love* your
money!

you never once said
you loved me!

what do you want
a liar or a
lover?

you're neither! out, bum,
out!

. . . but baby!

go back to O'Neill!

I went to the door,
softly closed it and walked away,
thinking: all they want
is a wooden Indian
to say yes and no
and stand over the fire and
not raise too much hell;
but you're getting to be
an old man, kiddo:
next time play it closer
to the
vest.

the twins

he hinted at times that I was a bastard and I told him to listen
to Brahms, and I told him to learn to paint and drink and not be
dominated by women and dollars
but he screamed at me, For Christ's sake remember your mother,
remember your country,
you'll kill us all! . . .

I move through my father's house (on which he owed $8,000 after 20
years on the same job) and look at his dead shoes
the way his feet curled the leather, as if he was angrily planting roses,
and he was, and I look at his dead cigarette, his last cigarette
and the last bed he slept in that night, and I feel I should remake it
but I can't, for a father is always your master even when he's gone;
I guess these things have happened time and again but I can't help
thinking

> to die on a kitchen floor at 7 o'clock in the morning
> while other people are frying eggs
> is not so rough
> unless it happens to you.

I go outside and pick an orange and peel back the bright skin;
things are still living: the grass is growing quite well,
the sun sends down its rays circled by a Russian satellite,
a dog barks senselessly somewhere, the neighbors peek behind blinds.
I am a stranger here, and have been (I suppose) somewhat the rogue,
and I have no doubt he painted me quite well (the old boy and I
fought like mountain lions) and they say he left it all to some woman
in Duarte but I don't give a damn—she can have it: he was my old

man
        and he died.

inside, I try on a light blue suit
much better than anything I have ever worn
and I flap the arms like a scarecrow in the wind
but it's no good:
I can't keep him alive
no matter how much we hated each other.

we looked exactly alike, we could have been twins
the old man and I: that's what they
said. he had his bulbs on the screen
ready for planting
while I was lying with a whore from 3rd Street.

very well. grant us this moment: standing before a mirror
in my dead father's suit
waiting also
to die.

to the whore who took my poems

some say we should keep personal remorse from the
poem,
stay abstract, and there is some reason in this,
but jezus:
12 poems gone and I don't keep carbons and you have
my
paintings too, my best ones; it's stifling:
are you trying to crush me out like the rest of them?
why didn't you take my money? they usually do
from the sleeping drunken pants sick in the corner.

next time take my left arm or a fifty
but not my poems:
I'm not Shakespeare
but sometimes simply
there won't be any more, abstract or otherwise;
there'll always be money and whores and drunkards
down to the last bomb,
but as God said,
crossing his legs,
I see where I have made plenty of poets
but not so very much
poetry.

the loser

and the next I remembered I'm on a table,
everybody's gone: the head of bravery
under light, scowling, flailing me down . . .
and then some toad stood there, smoking a cigar:
"Kid, you're no fighter," he told me,
and I got up and knocked him over a chair;
it was like a scene in a movie, and
he stayed there on his big rump and said
over and over: "Jesus, Jesus, whatsamatta wit
you?" and I got up and dressed,
the tape still on my hands, and when I got home
I tore the tape off my hands and
wrote my first poem,
and I've been fighting
ever since.

the best way to get famous is to run away

I found a loose cement slab outside the ice-cream store,
tossed it aside and began to dig; the earth was
soft and full of worms and soon I was in to my
waist, size 36;
a crowd gathered but stepped back before my shots
of mud,
and by the time the police came, I was in below
my head,
frightening gophers, eels and finding bits of golden
inlaid skull,
and they asked me, are you looking for oil, treasure,
gold, the end of China? are you looking for love, God,
a lost key chain? and little girls dripping ice-cream
peered into my darkness, and a psychiatrist came
and a
college professor and a movie actress in a bikini, and
a Russian spy and a French spy and an English spy,
and a drama critic and a bill collector and an old
girlfriend, and they all asked me, what are you
looking
for? and soon it began to rain . . . atomic submarines
changed course, Tuesday Weld hid behind a newspaper,
Jean-Paul Sartre rolled in his sleep, and my hole
filled
with water; I came out black as Africa, shooting
stars
and epitaphs, my pockets full of lovely worms,
and they took me to their jail and gave me a shower
and a nice cell, rent-free, and even now the people

are picketing in my cause, and I have signed
contracts to appear on the stage and television,
to write a guest column for the local paper and
write a book and endorse some products, I have
enough money to last me several years at the best
hotels, but as soon as I get out of here, I'm gonna
find me another loose slab and begin to dig, dig,
dig, and this time I'm not coming back . . . rain, shine,
or bikini, and the reporters keep asking, why did you
do it? but I just light my cigarette and smile . . .

the tragedy of the leaves

I awakened to dryness and the ferns were dead,
the potted plants yellow as corn;
my woman was gone
and the empty bottles like bled corpses
surrounded me with their uselessness;
the sun was still good, though,
and my landlady's note cracked in fine and
undemanding yellowness; what was needed now
was a good comedian, ancient style, a jester
with jokes upon absurd pain; pain is absurd
because it exists, nothing more;
I shaved carefully with an old razor
the man who had once been young and
said to have genius; but
that's the tragedy of the leaves,
the dead ferns, the dead plants;
and I walked into a dark hall
where the landlady stood
execrating and final,
sending me to hell,
waving her fat, sweaty arms
and screaming
screaming for rent
because the world had failed us
both.

Charles Bukowski
OLD MAN, DEAD
IN A ROOM

This thing upon me is not
death
but it's as real,
AND as LANDLORDS
full of MAGGOTS
pound FOR rent
I eat walnuts in the shell
of my privacy
and LISTEN FOR more important
drummers;
IT'S AS REAL, IT'S AS REAL
as the broken-boned SPARROW
cat-mouthed to utter
more than more
and miserable argument;
between my toes I STARE
at clouds, at seas of gaunt
sepulcher...
and scratch my BACK
and form a vowel
as all my LOVELY WOMEN
(WIVES AND LOVERS)
BREAK LIKE ENGINES
into some steam of sorrow
to be blown into ECLIPSE;
bone is bone
BONE IS BONE
but this thing UPON ME
LIKE A FLOWER/AND A FEAST,
BELEIVE me

is not death and is not
glory
and LIKE Quixote's WINDMILLS
makes a foe
turned by the HEAVENS
against one MAN;
...THIS THING upon ME,
great GOD,
THIS THING UPON ME
CRAWLING LIKE A SNAKE,
terrifying my love of
COMMONNESS,
some call ART
some call POETRY;
it's not DEATH
but dying DYING
WILL SOLVE it's POWER
and as my grey hands
drop a LAST
DESPERATE PEN
in some cheap ROOM
they will find me there
AND NEVER KNOW
my name
MY MEANING
nor the treasure
of my ESCAPE.

18

old man, dead in a room

this thing upon me is not death
but it's as real,
and as landlords full of maggots
pound for rent
I eat walnuts in the sheath
of my privacy
and listen for more important
drummers;
it's as real, it's as real
as the broken-boned sparrow
cat-mouthed to utter
more than mere
and miserable argument;
between my toes I stare
at clouds, at seas of gaunt
sepulcher . . .
and scratch my back
and form a vowel
as all my lovely women
(wives and lovers)
break like engines
into some steam of sorrow
to be blown into eclipse;
bone is bone
but this thing upon me
as I tear the window shades
and walk caged rugs,
this thing upon me
like a flower and a feast,

believe me
is not death and is not
glory
and like Quixote's windmills
makes a foe
turned by the heavens
against one man;
. . . this thing upon me,
great god,
this thing upon me
crawling like a snake,
terrifying my love of commonness,
some call Art
some call poetry;
it's not death
but dying will solve its power
and as my gray hands
drop a last desperate pen
in some cheap room
they will find me there
and never know
my name
my meaning
nor the treasure
of my escape.

the priest and the matador

in the slow Mexican air I watched the bull die
and they cut off his ear, and his great head held
no more terror than a rock.

driving back the next day we stopped at the Mission
and watched the golden red and blue flowers pulling
like tigers in the wind.

set this to metric: the bull, and the fort of Christ:
the matador on his knees, the dead bull his baby;
and the priest staring from the window
like a caged bear.

you may argue in the marketplace and pull at your
doubts with silken strings: I will only tell you
this: I have lived in both their temples,
believing all and nothing—perhaps, now, they will
die in mine.

the state of world affairs
from a 3rd floor window

I am watching a girl dressed in a
light green sweater, blue shorts, long black stockings;
there is a necklace of some sort
but her breasts are small, poor thing,
and she watches her nails
as her dirty white dog sniffs the grass
in erratic circles;
a pigeon is there too, circling,
half dead with a tick of a brain
and I am upstairs in my underwear,
3 day beard, pouring a beer and waiting
for something literary or symphonic to happen;
but they keep circling, circling, and a thin old man
in his last winter rolls by pushed by a girl
in a Catholic school dress;
somewhere there are the Alps, and ships
are now crossing the sea;
there are piles and piles of H- and A-bombs,
enough to blow up fifty worlds and Mars thrown in,
but they keep circling,
the girl shifts buttocks,
and the Hollywood Hills stand there, stand there
full of drunks and insane people and
much kissing in automobiles,
but it's no good: *che sarà, sarà:*
her dirty white dog simply will not shit,
and with a last look at her nails
she, with much whirling of buttocks

walks to her downstairs court
trailed by her constipated dog (simply not worried),
leaving me looking at a most unsymphonic pigeon.
well, from the looks of things, relax:
the bombs will
never
go off.

the swan

swans die in the spring too
and there it floated
dead on a Sunday
sideways
circling in current
and I walked to the rotunda
and overhead
gods in chariots
dogs, women
circled,
and death
ran down my throat
like a mouse,
and I heard the people coming
with their picnic bags
and laughter,
and I felt guilty
for the swan
as if death
were a thing of shame
and like a fool
I walked away
and left them
my beautiful swan.

beans with garlic

this is important enough:
to get your feelings down,
it is better than shaving
or cooking beans with garlic.
it is the little we can do
this small bravery of knowledge
and there is of course
madness and terror too
in knowing
that some part of you
wound up like a clock
can never be wound again
once it stops.
but now
there's a ticking under your shirt
and you whirl the beans with a spoon,
one love dead, one love departed
another love . . .
ah! as many loves as beans
yes, count them now
sad, sad
your feelings boiling over flame,
get this down.

a poem is a city

a poem is a city filled with streets and sewers
filled with saints, heroes, beggars, madmen,
filled with banality and booze,
filled with rain and thunder and periods of
drought, a poem is a city at war,
a poem is a city asking a clock why,
a poem is a city burning,
a poem is a city under guns
its barbershops filled with cynical drunks,
a poem is a city where God rides naked
through the streets like Lady Godiva,
where dogs bark at night, and chase away
the flag; a poem is a city of poets,
most of them quite similar
and envious and bitter . . .
a poem is this city now,
50 miles from nowhere,
9:09 in the morning,
the taste of liquor and cigarettes,
no police, no lovers walking the streets,
this poem, this city, closing its doors,
barricaded, almost empty,
mournful without tears, aging without pity,
the hardrock mountains,
the ocean like a lavender flame,
a moon destitute of greatness,
a small music from broken windows . . .

a poem is a city, a poem is a nation,
a poem is the world . . .

and now I stick this under glass
for the gaunt mad editor's scrutiny,
and night is elsewhere
and faint gray ladies stand in line,
dog follows dog to estuary,
the trumpets bring on gallows
as small men rant at things
they cannot do.

consummation of grief

I even hear the mountains
the way they laugh
up and down their blue sides
and down in the water
the fish cry
and all the water
is their tears.
I listen to the water
on nights I drink away
and the sadness becomes so great
I hear it in my clock
it becomes knobs upon my dresser
it becomes paper on the floor
it becomes a shoehorn
a laundry ticket
it becomes
cigarette smoke
climbing a chapel of dark vines . . .

it matters little

very little love is not so bad
or very little life

what counts
is waiting on walls
I was born for this

I was born to hustle roses down the avenues of the dead.

for Jane: with all the love I had,
which was not enough

I pick up the skirt,
I pick up the sparkling beads
in black,
this thing that moved once
around flesh,
and I call God a liar,
I say anything that moved
like that
or knew
my name
could never die
in the common verity of dying,
and I pick
up her lovely
dress,
all her loveliness gone,
and I speak
to all the gods,
Jewish gods, Christ-gods,
chips of blinking things,
idols, pills, bread,
fathoms, risks,
knowledgeable surrender,
rats in the gravy of 2 gone quite mad
without a chance,
hummingbird knowledge, hummingbird chance,
I lean upon this, ·
I lean on all of this

and I know:
her dress upon my arm:
but
they will not
give her back to me.

for Jane

225 days under grass
and you know more than I.

they have long taken your blood,
you are a dry stick in a basket.

is this how it works?

in this room
the hours of love
still make shadows.

when you left
you took almost
everything.

I kneel in the nights
before tigers
that will not let me be.

what you were
will not happen again.

the tigers have found me
and I do not care.

john dillinger and le chasseur maudit

it's unfortunate, and simply not the style, but I don't care:
girls remind me of hair in the sink, girls remind me of intestines
and bladders and excretory movements; it's unfortunate also that
ice-cream bells, babies, engine-valves, plagiostomes, palm trees,
footsteps in the hall . . . all excite me with the cold calmness
of the gravestone; nowhere, perhaps, is there sanctuary except
in hearing that there were other desperate men:
Dillinger, Rimbaud, Villon, Babyface Nelson, Seneca, Van Gogh,
or desperate women: lady wrestlers, nurses, waitresses, whores
poetesses . . . although,
I do suppose the breaking out of ice-cubes is important
or a mouse nosing an empty beercan—
two hollow emptinesses looking into each other,
or the nightsea stuck with soiled ships
that enter the chary web of your brain with their lights,
with their salty lights
that touch you and leave you
for the more solid love of some India;
or driving great distances without reason
sleep-drugged through open windows that
tear and flap your shirt like a frightened bird,
and always the stoplights, always red,
nightfire and defeat, defeat . . .
scorpions, scraps, fardels:
x-jobs, x-wives, x-faces, x-lives,
Beethoven in his grave as dead as a beet;
red wheel-barrows, yes, perhaps,
or a letter from Hell signed by the devil
or two good boys beating the guts out of each other

in some cheap stadium full of screaming smoke,
but mostly, I don't care, sitting here
with a mouthful of rotten teeth,
sitting here reading Herrick and Spenser and
Marvell and Hopkins and Bronte (Emily, today);
and listening to the Dvorak *Midday Witch*
or Franck's *Le Chasseur Maudit,*
actually I don't care, and it's unfortunate:
I have been getting letters from a young poet
(very young, it seems) telling me that some day
I will most surely be recognized as
one of the world's great poets. *Poet!*
a malversation: today I walked in the sun and streets
of this city: seeing nothing, learning nothing, being
nothing, and coming back to my room
I passed an old woman who smiled a horrible smile;
she was already dead, and everywhere I remembered wires:
telephone wires, electric wires, wires for electric faces
trapped like goldfish in the glass and smiling,
and the birds were gone, none of the birds wanted wire
or the smiling of wire
and I closed my door (at last)
but through the windows it was the same:
a horn honked, somebody laughed, a toilet flushed,
and oddly then
I thought of all the horses with numbers
that have gone by in the screaming,
gone by like Socrates, gone by like Lorca,
like Chatterton . . .

I'd rather imagine our death will not matter too much
except as a matter of disposal, a problem,
like dumping the garbage,
and although I have saved the young poet's letters,
I do not believe them
but like at the
diseased palm trees
and the end of the sun,
I sometimes look.

crucifix in a deathhand

yes, they begin out in a willow, I think
the starch mountains begin out in the willow
and keep right on going without regard for
pumas or nectarines
somehow these mountains are like
an old woman with a bad memory and
a shopping basket.
we are in a basin, that is the
idea. down in the sand and the alleys,
this land punched-in, cuffed-out, divided,
held like a crucifix in a deathhand,
this land bought, resold, bought again and
sold again, the wars long over,
the Spaniards all the way back in Spain
down in the thimble again, and now
real estaters, subdividers, landlords, freeway
engineers arguing. this is their land and
I walk on it, live on it a little while
near Hollywood here I see young men in rooms
listening to glazed recordings
and I think too of old men sick of music
sick of everything, and death like suicide
I think is sometimes voluntary, and to get your
hold on the land here it is best to return to the
Grand Central Market, see the old Mexican women,
the poor . . . I am sure you have seen these same women
many years before
arguing
with the same young Japanese clerks
witty, knowledgeable and golden

among their soaring store of oranges, apples
avocados, tomatoes, cucumbers—
and you know how *these* look, they do look good
as if you could eat them all
light a cigar and smoke away the bad world.
then it's best to go back to the bars, the same bars—
wooden, stale, merciless, green
with the young policeman walking through
scared and looking for trouble,
and the beer is still bad
it has an edge that already mixes with vomit and
decay, and you've got to be strong in the shadows
to ignore it, to ignore the poor and to ignore yourself
and the shopping bag between your legs
down there feeling good with its avocados and
oranges and fresh fish and wine bottles, who needs
a Fort Lauderdale winter?
25 years ago there used to be a whore there
with a film over one eye, who was too fat
and made little silver bells out of cigarette
tinfoil. the sun seemed warmer then
although this was probably not
true, and you take your shopping bag
outside and walk along the street
and the green beer hangs there
just above your stomach like
a short and shameful shawl, and
you look around and no longer
see any
old men.

CRUCIFIX IN A DEATHHAND

YES, THEY BEGIN OUT IN THE WILLOW, I THINK
THE STARCH MOUNTAINS BEGIN OUT IN THE WILLOW
AND KEEP RIGHT ON GOING WITHOUT REGARD FOR
PUMAS OR NECTARINES
SOMEHOW THESE MOUNTAINS ARE LIKE AN OLD WOMAN
WITH A BAD MEMORY AND A SHOPPING
BASKET. WE ARE IN THE BASIN. THAT IS THE
IDEA. DOWN IN THE SAND AND THE ALLEYS,
THIS LAND PUNCHED-IN, CUFFED-OUT, DIVIDED,
HELD LIKE A CRUCIFIX IN A DEATHHAND,
THIS LAND BOUGHT, RESOLD, BOUGHT AGAIN AND
SOLD AGAIN, THE WARS LONG OVER,
THE SPANIARDS ALL THE WAY BACK IN SPAIN
DOWN IN THE THIMBLE AGAIN, AND NOW
REAL ESTATERS, SUBDIVIDERS, LANDLORDS, FREEWAY
ENGINEERS ARGUING. THIS IS THEIR LAND AND
I WALK ON IT, LIVE ON IT A LITTLE WHILE
NEAR HOLLYWOOD HERE WHERE I SEE YOUNG MEN IN ROOMS
LISTENING TO GLAZED RECORDINGS
AND I THINK TOO OF OLD MEN SICK OF MUSIC
SICK OF EVERYTHING, AND DEATH LIKE SUICIDE
I THINK IS SOMETIMES VOLUNTARY, AND TO GET YOUR
HOLD ON THE LAND HERE IT IS BEST TO RETURN TO THE
GRAND CENTRAL MARKET, SEE THE OLD MEXICAN WOMEN
THE POOR... I AM SURE YOU HAVE SEEN THESE SAME WOMEN
MANY YEARS BEFORE
ARGUING
WITH THE SAME YOUNG JAPANESE CLERKS
WITTY, KNOWLEDGEABLE AND GOLDEN
AMONG THEIR SOARING STORE OF ORANGES, APPLES,
AVOCADOES, TOMATOES, CUCUMBERS—
AND YOU KNOW HOW THESE LOOK, THEY DO LOOK GOOD
AS IF YOU COULD EAT THEM ALL
LIGHT A CIGAR AND SMOKE AWAY THE BAD WORLD.
THEN IT'S BEST TO GO BACK TO THE BARS, THE SAME BARS—
WOODEN, STALE, MERCILESS, GREEN
WITH THE YOUNG POLICEMAN HUNTING THROUGH
SCARED AND LOOKING FOR TROUBLE
AND THE BEER IS STILL BAD,
IT HAS AN EDGE THAT ALREADY MIXES WITH VOMIT AND
DECAY, AND YOU'VE GOT TO BE STRONG IN THE SHADOWS →
TO IGNORE IT, TO IGNORE THE POOR AND TO IGNORE YOURSELF
AND THE SHOPPING BAG BETWEEN YOUR LEGS
DOWN THERE FEELING GOOD WITH ITS AVOCADOES AND ORANGES AND
FRESH FISH AND WINE BOTTLE, WHO NEEDS A FORT LAUDERDALE WINTER?
25 YEARS AGO THERE USED TO BE A WHORE THERE WITH A
FILM OVER ONE EYE, WHO WAS TOO FAT AND MADE LITTLE SILVER BELLS
OUT OF CIGARETTE TINFOIL. THE SUN SEEMED WARMER THEN
ALTHOUGH THIS WAS PROBABLY NOT
TRUE, AND YOU
TAKE YOUR SHOPPING BAG OUTSIDE AND WALK ALONG THE STREET
AND THE GREEN BEER HANGS THERE JUST ABOVE YOUR STOMACH LIKE
A SHORT AND SHAMEFUL SHAWL, AND
YOU LOOK AROUND AND NO LONGER
SEE ANY
OLD MEN.

Charles Bukowski

```
something for the
touts, the nuns, the
grocery clerks
and you . . .
```

we have everything and we have nothing
and some men do it in churches
and some men do it by tearing butterflies
in half
and some men do it in Palm Springs
laying it into butterblondes
with Cadillac souls
Cadillacs and butterflies
nothing and everything,
the face melting down to the last puff
in a cellar in Corpus Christi.
there's something for the touts, the nuns,
the grocery clerks and you . . .
something at 8 a.m., something in the library
something in the river,
everything and nothing.
in the slaughterhouse it comes running along
the ceiling on a hook, and you swing it—
one
    two
        three
and then you've got it, $200 worth of dead
meat, its bones against your bones
something and nothing.
it's always early enough to die and
it's always too late,

and the drill of blood in the basin white
it tells you nothing at all
and the gravediggers playing poker over
5 a.m. coffee, waiting for the grass
to dismiss the frost . . .
they tell you nothing at all.

we have everything and we have nothing—
days with glass edges and the impossible stink
of river moss—worse than shit;
checkerboard days of moves and countermoves,
fagged interest, with as much sense in defeat as
in victory; slow days like mules
humping it slagged and sullen and sun-glazed
up a road where a madman sits waiting among
bluejays and wrens netted in and sucked a flakey
gray.
good days too of wine and shouting, fights
in alleys, fat legs of women striving around
your bowels buried in moans,
the signs in bullrings like diamonds hollering
Mother Capri, violets coming out of the ground
telling you to forget the dead armies and the loves
that robbed you.
days when children say funny and brilliant things
like savages trying to send you a message through
their bodies while their bodies are still
alive enough to transmit and feel and run up
and down without locks and paychecks and

ideals and possessions and beetle-like
opinions.
days when you can cry all day long in
a green room with the door locked, days
when you can laugh at the breadman
because his legs are too long, days
of looking at hedges . . .

and nothing, and nothing. the days of
the bosses, yellow men
with bad breath and big feet, men
who look like frogs, hyenas, men who walk
as if melody had never been invented, men
who think it is intelligent to hire and fire and
profit, men with expensive wives they possess
like 60 acres of ground to be drilled
or shown-off or to be walled away from
the incompetent, men who'd kill you
because they're crazy and justify it because
it's the law, men who stand in front of
windows 30 feet wide and see nothing,
men with luxury yachts who can sail around
the world and yet never get out of their vest
pockets, men like snails, men like eels, men
like slugs, and not as good . . .

and nothing. getting your last paycheck
at a harbor, at a factory, at a hospital, at an
aircraft plant, at a penny arcade, at a

barbershop, at a job you didn't want
anyway.
income tax, sickness, servility, broken
arms, broken heads—all the stuffing
comes out like an old pillow.

we have everything and we have nothing.
some do it well enough for a while and
then give way. fame gets them or disgust
or age or lack of proper diet or ink
across the eyes or children in college
or new cars or broken backs while skiing
in Switzerland or new politics or new wives
or just natural change and decay—
the man you knew yesterday hooking
for ten rounds or drinking for three days and
three nights by the Sawtooth mountains now
just something under a sheet or a cross
or a stone or under an easy delusion,
or packing a Bible or a golf bag or a
briefcase: how they go, how they go!—all
the ones you thought would never go.

days like this. like your day today.
maybe the rain on the window trying to
get through to you. what do you see today?
what is it? where are you? the best
days are sometimes the first, sometimes
the middle and even sometimes the last.

the vacant lots are not bad. churches in
Europe on postcards are not bad. people in
wax museums frozen into their best sterility
are not bad, horrible but not bad. the
cannon, think of the cannon. and toast for
breakfast the coffee hot enough you
know your tongue is still there. three
geraniums outside a window, trying to be
red and trying to be pink and trying to be
geraniums. no wonder sometimes the women
cry, no wonder the mules don't want
to go up the hill. are you in a hotel room
in Detroit looking for a cigarette? one more
good day. a little bit of it. and as
the nurses come out of the building after
their shift, having had enough, eight nurses
with different names and different places
to go—walking across the lawn, some of them
want cocoa and a paper, some of them want a
hot bath, some of them want a man, some
of them are hardly thinking at all. enough
and not enough. arcs and pilgrims, oranges
gutters, ferns, antibodies, boxes of
tissue paper.

in the most decent sometimes sun
there is the softsmoke feeling from urns
and the canned sound of old battleplanes
and if you go inside and run your finger

along the window ledge you'll find
dirt, maybe even earth.
and if you look out the window
there will be the day, and as you
get older you'll keep looking
keep looking
sucking your tongue in a little
ah ah   no no   maybe

some do it naturally
some obscenely
everywhere.

no. 6

I'll settle for the 6 horse
on a rainy afternoon
a paper cup of coffee
in my hand
a little way to go,
the wind twirling out
small wrens from
the upper grandstand roof,
the jocks coming out
for a middle race
silent
and the easy rain making
everything
at once
almost alike,
the horses at peace with
each other
before the drunken war
and I am under the grandstand
feeling for
cigarettes
settling for coffee,
then the horses walk by
taking their little men
away—
it is funereal and graceful
and glad
like the opening
of flowers.

and the moon and the stars and the world:

long walks at
night—
that's what's good
for the
soul:
peeking into windows
watching tired
housewives
trying to fight
off
their beer-maddened
husbands.

true story

they found him walking along the freeway
all red in
front
he had taken a rusty tin can
and cut off his sexual
machinery
as if to say—
see what you've done to
me? you might as well have the
rest.

and he put part of him
in one pocket and
part of him in
another
and that's how they found him,
walking
along.

they gave him over to the
doctors
who tried to sew the parts
back
on
but the parts were
quite contented
the way they
were.

I think sometimes of all the good
ass
turned over to the
monsters of the
world.

maybe it was his protest against
this or
his protest
against
everything.

a one man
Freedom March
that never squeezed in
between
the concert reviews and the
baseball
scores.

God, or somebody,
bless
him.

the genius of the crowd

There is enough treachery, hatred,
                    violence,
Absurdity in the average human
                    being
To supply any given army on any given
          day.
AND The Best At Murder Are Those
          Who Preach Against It.
AND The Best At Hate Are Those
          Who Preach LOVE
AND THE BEST AT WAR
—FINALLY—ARE THOSE WHO
PREACH
                    PEACE

Those Who Preach GOD
                    NEED God
Those Who Preach PEACE
                    Do Not Have Peace.
THOSE WHO PREACH LOVE
                    DO NOT HAVE LOVE
BEWARE THE PREACHERS
Beware The Knowers.

          Beware
          Those Who
          Are ALWAYS
          READING
          BOOKS

Beware Those Who Either Detest
         Poverty Or Are Proud Of It

BEWARE Those Quick To Praise
For They Need PRAISE In Return
BEWARE Those Quick To Censure:
They Are Afraid Of What They Do
Not Know

Beware Those Who Seek Constant
Crowds; They Are Nothing
Alone

         Beware
         The Average Man
         The Average Woman
         BEWARE Their Love

Their Love Is Average, Seeks
Average
But There Is Genius In Their Hatred
There Is Enough Genius In Their
Hatred To Kill You, To Kill
Anybody.

Not Wanting Solitude
Not Understanding Solitude
They Will Attempt To Destroy
Anything

That Differs
From Their Own

        Not Being Able
        To Create Art
        They Will Not
        Understand Art

They Will Consider Their Failure
As Creators
Only As A Failure
Of The World

Not Being Able To Love Fully
They Will BELIEVE Your Love
Incomplete
AND THEN THEY WILL HATE
YOU

And Their Hatred Will Be Perfect
Like A Shining Diamond
Like A Knife
Like A Mountain
LIKE A TIGER
LIKE Hemlock
        Their Finest
        ART

I met a genius

I met a genius on the train
today
about 6 years old,
he sat beside me
and as the train
ran down along the coast
we came to the ocean
and then he looked at me
and said,
"it's not pretty."

it was the first time I'd
realized
that.

swastika star buttoned to my ass

sitting around here burning spiders to death with my
cigar
I can hardly believe that all your pussies are as
sweet as mine used to
be.
I did it in fireplaces
on fire escapes
in cornfields
in mother's bedroom (with mother) (sometimes)
between bomb explosions at Nantes and St. Etienne
over the sink of the men's crapper
in a train passing through Utah.
I've done it sober
potted
crazy and sane.
I've done it when I wanted to and when I haven't wanted
to.
I've done it with women twice my age and with women half my
age.
I've done it with animals, I've done it with dead meat:
beefsteak and melted butter and I've used my
hand.

now the only things that stand up around here
are the rods that hold up the
lampshades. I am going to rob a bank or beat hell out of a
blind man any day now and they'll never know
why.

the blackbirds are rough today

lonely as a dry and used orchard
spread over the earth
for use and surrender.

shot down like an ex-pug selling
dailies on the corner.

taken by tears like
an aging chorus girl
who has gotten her last check.

a hanky is in order your lord your
worship.

the blackbirds are rough today
like
ingrown toenails
in an overnight
jail—
wine wine whine,
the blackbirds run around and
fly around
harping about
Spanish melodies and bones.

and everywhere is
nowhere—
the dream is as bad as
flapjacks and flat tires:

why do we go on
with our minds and
pockets full of
dust
like a bad boy just out of
school—
you tell
me,
you who were a hero in some
revolution
you who teach children
you who drink with calmness
you who own large homes
and walk in gardens
you who have killed a man and own a
beautiful wife
you tell me
why I am on fire like old dry
garbage.

we might surely have some interesting
correspondence.
it will keep the mailman busy.
and the butterflies and ants and bridges and
cemeteries
the rocket-makers and dogs and garage mechanics
will still go on a
while
until we run out of stamps

and/or
ideas.

don't be ashamed of
anything; I guess God meant it all
like
locks on
doors.

if we take—

if we take what we can see—
the engines driving us mad,
lovers finally hating;
this fish in the market
staring upward into our minds;
flowers rotting, flies web-caught;
riots, roars of caged lions,
clowns in love with dollar bills,
nations moving people like pawns;
daylight thieves with beautiful
nighttime wives and wines;
the crowded jails,
the commonplace unemployed,
dying grass, 2-bit fires;
men old enough to love the grave.

these things, and others, in content
show life swinging on a rotten axis.

but they've left us a bit of music
and a spiked show in the corner,
a jigger of scotch, a blue necktie,
a small volume of poems by Rimbaud,
a horse running as if the devil were
twisting his tail
over bluegrass and screaming, and then,
love again
like a streetcar turning the corner
on time,

the city waiting,
the wine and the flowers,
the water walking across the lake
and summer and winter and summer and summer
and winter again.

another academy

how can they go on, you see them
sitting in old doorways
with dirty stained caps and thick clothes and
no place to go;
heads bent down, arms on
knees they
wait.
or they stand in front of the Mission
700 of them
quiet as oxen
waiting to be let into the chapel
where they will sleep upright on the hard benches
leaning against each other
snoring and
dreaming;
men
without.

in New York City
where it gets colder
and they are hunted by their own
kind, these men often crawl under car radiators,
drink the antifreeze,
get warm and grateful for some minutes, then
die.

but that is an older
culture and a wiser
one;

here they scratch and
wait,
while on Sunset Boulevard the
hippies and yippies
hitchhike in
$50
boots.

out in front of the Mission I heard one guy say to
another:
"John Wayne won it."
"Won what?" said the other guy
tossing the last of his rolled cigarette into the
street.

I thought that was
rather good.

the poetry reading

at high noon
at a small college near the beach
sober
the sweat running down my arms
a spot of sweat on the table
I flatten it with my finger
blood money blood money
my god they must think I love this like the others
but it's for bread and beer and rent
blood money
I'm tense   lousy   feel bad
poor people   I'm failing   I'm failing

a woman gets up
walks out
slams the door

a dirty poem
somebody told me not to read dirty poems
here

it's too late.

my eyes can't see some lines
I read it
out—
desperate trembling
lousy

they can't hear my voice
and I say,
I quit, that's it, I'm
finished.

and later in my room
there's scotch and beer:
the blood of a
coward.

this then
will be my destiny:
scrabbling for pennies in dark tiny halls
reading poems I have long since become tired
of.

and I used to think
that men who drove buses
or cleaned out latrines
or murdered men in alleys were
fools.

the last days of the suicide kid

I can see myself now
after all these suicide days and nights,
being pushed out of one of those sterile rest homes
(of course, this is only if I get famous and lucky)
by a subnormal and bored nurse . . .
there I am sitting upright in my wheelchair . . .
almost blind, eyes rolling backward into the dark part of my skull
looking
for the mercy of death . . .

"Isn't it a lovely day, Mr. Bukowski?"

"O, yeah, yeah . . ."

the children walk past and I don't even exist
and lovely women walk by
with big hot hips
and warm buttocks and tight hot everything
praying to be loved
and I don't even
exist . . .

"It's the first sunlight we've had in 3 days,
Mr. Bukowski."

"O, yeah, yeah."

there I am sitting upright in my wheelchair,
myself whiter than this sheet of paper,

bloodless,
brain gone, gamble gone, me, Bukowski,
gone . . .

"Isn't it a lovely day, Mr. Bukowski?"

"O, yeah, yeah . . ." pissing in my pajamas, slop drooling out of my
mouth.

2 young schoolboys run by—

"Hey, did you see that old guy?"

"Christ, yes, he made me sick!"

after all the threats to do so
somebody else has committed suicide for me
at last.

the nurse stops the wheelchair, breaks a rose from a nearby bush,
puts it in my
hand.

I don't even know
what it is. it might as well be my pecker
for all the good
it does.

the shower

we like to shower afterwards
(I like the water hotter than she)
and her face is always soft and peaceful
and she'll wash me first
spread the soap over my balls
lift the balls
squeeze them,
then wash the cock:
"hey, this thing is still hard!"
then get all the hair down there—
the belly, the back, the neck, the legs,
I grin grin grin,
and then I wash her . . .
first the cunt, I
stand behind her, my cock in the cheeks of her ass
I gently soap up the cunt hairs,
wash there with a soothing motion,
I linger perhaps longer than necessary,
then I get the backs of the legs, the ass,
the back, the neck, I turn her, kiss her,
soap up the breasts, get them and the belly, the neck,
the fronts of the legs, the ankles, the feet,
and then the cunt, once more, for luck . . .
another kiss, and she gets out first,
toweling, sometimes singing while I stay in
turn the water on hotter
feeling the good times of love's miracle
I then get out . . .
it is usually mid-afternoon and quiet,

and getting dressed we talk about what else
there might be to do,
but being together solves most of it,
in fact, solves all of it
for as long as those things stay solved
in the history of woman and
man, it's different for each
better and worse for each—
for me, it's splendid enough to remember
past the marching of armies
and the horses that walk the streets outside
past the memories of pain and defeat and unhappiness:
Linda, you brought it to me,
when you take it away
do it slowly and easily
make it as if I were dying in my sleep instead of in
my life, amen.

The Mockingbird

the mockingbird has been following the cat
all summer
mocking mocking mocking
teasing,
~~avaricious~~ and cocksure;
the cat crawled under rockers on porches
tail flashing
and he said something very angry to the mockingbird
which I didn't understand.
~~of course, the bird was protecting its nest~~
~~I understood~~

yesterday the cat walked calmly up the driveway
with the mockingbird alive in its mouth,
wings fanned, beautiful wings fanned and flopping,
feathers parted like a woman's legs in sex,
and the bird was no longer mocking,
it was asking, it was praying
but the cat
striding down through centuries
would not listen.

I saw it crawl under a yellow car
with the bird
to bargain it to another place.

summer was over.

Charles Bukowski (signature)

the mockingbird

the mockingbird had been following the cat
all summer
mocking mocking mocking
teasing and cocksure;
the cat crawled under rockers on porches
tail flashing
and said something very angry to the mockingbird
which I didn't understand.

yesterday the cat walked calmly up the driveway
with the mockingbird alive in its mouth,
wings fanned, beautiful wings fanned and flopping,
feathers parted like a woman's legs in sex,
and the bird was no longer mocking,
it was asking, it was praying
but the cat
striding down through centuries
would not listen.

I saw it crawl under a yellow car
with the bird
to bargain it to another place.

summer was over.

style

style is the answer to everything—
a fresh way to approach a dull or a
dangerous thing.
to do a dull thing with style
is preferable to doing a dangerous thing
without it.

Joan of Arc had style
John the Baptist
Christ
Socrates
Caesar,
García Lorca.

style is the difference,
a way of doing,
a way of being done.

6 herons standing quietly in a pool of water
or you walking out of the bathroom naked
without seeing
me.

girl in a miniskirt reading the Bible
outside my window

Sunday. I am eating a
grapefruit. church is over at the Russian
Orthodox to the
west.
she is dark
of Eastern descent,
large brown eyes look up from the Bible
then down. a small red and black
Bible, and as she reads
her legs keep moving, moving,
she is doing a slow rhythmic dance
reading the Bible . . .
long gold earrings;
2 gold bracelets on each arm,
and it's a mini-*suit*, I suppose,
the cloth covers her body,
the lightest of tans is that cloth,
she twists this way and that,
long young legs warm in the sun . . .

there is no escaping her being
there is no desire to . . .
my radio is playing symphonic music
that she cannot hear
but her movements coincide *exactly*
to the rhythms of the
symphony . . .

she is dark, she is dark
she is reading about God.

I am God.

the shoelace

a woman, a tire that's flat, a
disease, a
desire; fears in front of you,
fears that hold so still
you can study them
like pieces on a
chessboard . . .
it's not the large things that
send a man to a
madhouse . . . death he's ready for, or
murder, incest, robbery, fire, flood . . .
no, it's the continuing series of *small* tragedies
that send a man to the
madhouse . . .
not the death of his love
but a shoelace that snaps
with no time left . . .
the dread of life
is that huge swarm of trivial shit
that can kill quicker than cancer
and which is always there—
license plates or taxes
or expired driver's license,
or hiring or firing,
doing it or having it done to you, or
farts or constipation
or speeding tickets
or rickets or crickets or mice or termites or

roaches or flies or a
broken hook on a
screen, or out of gas
or too much gas,
the sink's stopped-up, the landlord's drunk,
the president doesn't care and the governor's
crazy.
lightswitch broken, mattress like a porcupine;
$105 for a tune-up, carburetor and fuel pump at
Sears Roebuck;
and the phone bill's up and the market's
down
and the toilet chain is broken,
and the light has burned out—
the hall light, the front light, the back light,
the inner light; it's
darker than hell
and twice as
expensive.
then there's always crabs and ingrown toenails
and people who insist they're
your friends;
there's always that and worse:
clap, Christ and Christmas;
blue salami, 9 day rains,
50 cent avocados
and purple
liverwurst.

or making it
as a waitress at Norm's on the split shift,
or as an emptier of
bedpans,
or as a carwash or a busboy
or a stealer of old lady's purses
leaving them screaming on the sidewalks
with broken arms at the age of
80.

suddenly
2 red lights in your rear view mirror
and blood in your
underwear;
and toothache, and $979 for a bridge
$300 for a gold
tooth,
and China and Russia and America, and
long hair and short hair and no
hair, and beards and no
beards, and faces and no
faces, and plenty of *zigzag* but no
pot, except maybe one to piss in and
the other one around your
gut.

with each broken shoelace
out of one hundred broken shoelaces,
one man, one woman, one

thing
enters a
madhouse.

so be careful
when you
bend over.

those sons of bitches

the dead come running sideways
holding toothpaste ads,
the dead are drunk on New Year's Eve
satisfied at Christmas
thankful on Thanksgiving
bored on the 4th of July
loafing on Labor Day
confused at Easter
cloudy at funerals
clowning at hospitals
nervous at birth;
the dead shop for stockings and shorts
and belts and rugs and vases and
coffeetables,
the dead dance with the dead
the dead sleep with the dead
the dead eat with the dead.

the dead get hungry looking at hogs' heads.

the dead get rich
the dead get deader

those sons of bitches

this graveyard above the ground

one tombstone for the mess,
I say:
humanity, you never had it
from the beginning.

hot

she was hot, she was so hot
I didn't want anybody else to have her,
and if I didn't get home on time
she'd be gone, and I couldn't bear that—
I'd go mad . . .
it was foolish I know, childish,
but I was caught in it, I was caught.

I delivered all the mail
and then Henderson put me on the night pickup run
in an old army truck,
the damn thing began to heat halfway through the run
and the night went on
me thinking about my hot Miriam
and jumping in and out of the truck
filling mailsacks
the engine continuing to heat up
the temperature needle was at the top
HOT HOT
like Miriam.

I leaped in and out
3 more pickups and into the station
I'd be, my car
waiting to get me to Miriam who sat on my blue couch
with scotch on the rocks
crossing her legs and swinging her ankles
like she did,
2 more stops . . .

the truck stalled at a traffic light, it was hell
kicking it over
again . . .
I had to be home by 8, 8 was the deadline for Miriam.

I made the last pickup and the truck stalled at a signal
½ block from the station . . .
it wouldn't start, it couldn't start . . .
I locked the doors, pulled the key and ran down to the
station . . .
I threw the keys down . . . signed out . . .
"your god damned truck is stalled at the signal,
Pico and Western . . ."

. . . I ran down the hall, put the key into the door,
opened it . . . her drinking glass was there, and a note:

> *sun of a bitch*
>
> *I wated until 5 after ate*
>
> *you don't love me*
>
> *you sun of a bitch*
>
> *somebody will love me*
>
> *I been wateing all day*
> *Miriam*

I poured a drink and let the water run into the tub
there were 5,000 bars in town
and I'd make 25 of them
looking for Miriam

her purple teddy bear held the note
as he leaned against a pillow

I gave the bear a drink, myself a drink
and got into the hot
water.

trouble with Spain

I got in the shower
and burned my balls
last Wednesday.

met this painter called Spain,
no, he was a cartoonist,
well, I met him at a party
and everybody got mad at me
because I didn't know who he was
or what he did.

he was rather a handsome guy
and I guess he was jealous because
I was so ugly.
they told me his name
and he was leaning against the wall
looking handsome, and I said:
"hey, Spain, I like that name: Spain
but I don't like you. why don't we step out
in the garden and I'll kick the shit out of your
ass?"

this made the hostess angry
and she walked over and rubbed his pecker
while I went to the crapper
and heaved.

but everybody's angry at me.
Bukowski, he can't write, he's had it.

washed-up. look at him drink.
he never used to come to parties.
now he comes to parties and drinks everything
up and insults real talent.
I used to admire him when he cut his wrists
and when he tried to kill himself with
gas. look at him now leering at that 19 year old
girl, and you know he
can't get it up.

I not only burnt my balls in that shower
last Wednesday, I spun around to get out of the burning
water and burnt my bunghole
too.

a radio with guts

it was on the 2nd floor on Coronado Street
I used to get drunk
and throw the radio through the window
while it was playing, and, of course,
it would break the glass in the window
and the radio would sit out there on the roof
still playing
and I'd tell my woman,
"Ah, what a marvelous radio!"

the next morning I'd take the window
off the hinges
and carry it down the street
to the glass man
who would put in another pane.

I kept throwing that radio through the window
each time I got drunk
and it would sit out there on the roof
still playing—
a most magic radio
a radio with guts,
and each morning I'd take the window
back to the glass man.

I don't remember how it ended exactly
though I do remember
we finally moved out.
there was a woman downstairs who worked in

the garden in her bathing suit
and her husband complained he couldn't sleep nights
because of me
so we moved out
and in the next place
I either forgot to throw the radio out the window
or I didn't feel like it
anymore.

I do remember missing the woman who worked in the
garden in her bathing suit,
she really dug with that trowel
and she put her behind up in the air
and I used to sit in the window
and watch the sun shine all over that thing

while the music played.

love poem to Marina

my girl is 8
and that's old enough to know
better or worse or
anything
so I relax around her and
hear various astounding things
about sex
life in general and life in particular;
mostly it's very
easy
except I became a father when most men
become grandfathers, I am a very late starter
in everything,
and I stretch on the grass and sand
and she rips dandelions up
and places them in my
hair
while I doze in the sea breeze.
I awaken
shake
say, "what the hell?"
and flowers fall over my eyes and over my nose
and over my lips.
I brush them away
and she sits above me
giggling.

daughter,
right or wrong,

I do love you,
it's only that sometimes I act as if
you weren't there,
but there have been fights with women
notes left on dressers
factory jobs
flat tires in Compton at 3 a.m.,
all those things that keep people from
knowing each other and
worse than
that.

thanks for the
flowers.

some people never go crazy

some people never go crazy.
me, sometimes I'll lie down behind the couch
for 3 or 4 days.
they'll find me there.
it's Cherub, they'll say, and
pour wine down my throat
rub my chest
sprinkle me with oils.

then I'll rise with a roar,
rant, rage—
curse them and the universe
as I send them scattering over the
lawn.
I'll feel much better,
sit down to toast and eggs,
hum a little tune,
suddenly become as lovable as a
pink
overfed whale.

some people never go crazy.
what truly horrible lives
they must live.

the fisherman

he comes out at 7:30 a.m. every day
with 3 peanut butter sandwiches, and
there's one can of beer
which he floats in the baitbucket.
he fishes for hours with a small trout pole
three-quarters of the way down the pier.
he's 75 years old and the sun doesn't tan him,
and no matter how hot it gets
the brown and green lumberjack stays on.
he catches starfish, baby sharks, and mackerel;
he catches them by the dozen,
speaks to nobody.
sometime during the day
he drinks his can of beer.
at 6 p.m. he gathers his gear and his catch
walks down the pier
across several streets
where he enters a small Santa Monica apartment
goes to the bedroom and opens the evening paper
as his wife throws the starfish, the sharks, the mackerel
into the garbage.

he lights his pipe
and waits for dinner.

the trash men

here they come
these guys
gray truck
radio playing

they are in a hurry

it's quite exciting:
shirt open
bellies hanging out

they run out the trash bins
roll them out to the fork lift
and then the truck grinds it upward
with far too much sound . . .

they had to fill out application forms
to get these jobs
they are paying for homes and
drive late model cars

they get drunk on Saturday night

now in the Los Angeles sunshine
they run back and forth with their trash bins

all that trash goes somewhere

and they shout to each other

then they are all up in the truck
driving west toward the sea

none of them know
that I am alive

REX DISPOSAL CO.

face of a political candidate on
a street billboard

there he is:
not too many hangovers
not too many fights with women
not too many flat tires
never a thought of suicide

not more than three toothaches
never missed a meal
never in jail
never in love

4 pairs of shoes

a son in college

a car one year old

insurance policies

a very green lawn

garbage cans with tight lids

he'll be elected.

the proud
thin
dying

I see old people on pensions in the
supermarkets and they are thin and they are
proud and they are dying
they are starving on their feet and saying
nothing. long ago, among other lies,
they were taught that silence was
bravery. now, having worked a lifetime,
inflation has trapped them. they look around
steal a grape
chew on it. finally they make a tiny
purchase, a day's worth.
another lie they were taught:
thou shalt not steal.
they'd rather starve than steal
(one grape won't save them)
and in tiny rooms
while reading the market ads
they'll starve
they'll die without a sound
pulled out of roominghouses
by young blond boys with long hair
who'll slide them in
and pull away from the curb, these
boys
handsome of eye

thinking of Vegas and pussy and
victory.
it's the order of things: each one
gets a taste of honey
then the knife.

an almost made up poem

I see you drinking at a fountain with tiny
blue hands, no, your hands are not tiny
they are small, and the fountain is in France
where you wrote me that last letter and
I answered and never heard from you again.
you used to write insane poems about
ANGELS AND GOD, all in upper case, and you
knew famous artists and most of them
were your lovers, and I wrote back, it's all right,
go ahead, enter their lives, I'm not jealous
because we've never met. we got close once in
New Orleans, one half block, but never met, never
touched. so you went with the famous and wrote
about the famous, and, of course, what you found out
is that the famous are worried about
their fame—not the beautiful young girl in bed
with them, who gives them *that,* and then awakens
in the morning to write upper case poems about
ANGELS AND GOD. we know God is dead, they've told
us, but listening to you I wasn't sure. maybe
it was the upper case. you were one of the
best female poets alive and I told some of the
editors, "print her, print her, she's mad but she's
magic. there's no lie in her fire." I loved you
like a man loves a woman he never touches, only
writes to, keeps little photographs of. I would have
loved you more if I had sat in a small room rolling a
cigarette and listened to you piss in the bathroom,
but that didn't happen. your letters got sadder.

your lovers betrayed you. kid, I wrote back, all
lovers betray. it didn't help. you said
you had a crying bench and it was by a bridge and
the bridge was over a river and you sat on the crying
bench every night and wept for the lovers who had
hurt and forgotten you. I wrote back but never
heard again. a friend wrote me of your suicide
3 or 4 months after it happened. if I had met you
I would probably have been unfair to you or you
to me. it was best like this.

a love poem for all the women I have known

all the women
all their kisses the
different ways they love and
talk and need.

their ears they all have
ears and
throats and dresses
and shoes and
automobiles and ex-
husbands.

mostly
the women are very
warm they remind me of
buttered toast with the butter
melted
in.

there is a look in the
eye: they have been
taken they have been
fooled. I don't know quite what to
do for
them.

I am
a fair cook a good
listener

but I never learned to
dance—I was busy
then with larger things.

but I've enjoyed their different
beds
smoking cigarettes
staring at the
ceilings. I was neither vicious nor
unfair. only
a student.

I know they all have these
feet and barefoot they go across the floor as
I watch their bashful buttocks in the
dark. I know that they like me, some even
love me
but I love very
few.

some give me oranges and pills;
others talk quietly of
childhood and fathers and
landscapes; some are almost
crazy but none of them are without
meaning; some love
well, others not
so; the best at sex are not always the
best in other

ways; each has limits as I have
limits and we learn
each other
quickly.

all the women all the
women all the
bedrooms
the rugs the
photos the
curtains, it's
something like a church only
at times there's
laughter.

those ears those
arms those
elbows those eyes
looking the fondness and
the waiting I have been
held I have been
held.

art

as the
spirit
wanes
the
form
appears.

what they want

Vallejo writing about ultimate
loneliness while starving to
death;
Van Gogh's ear rejected by a
whore;
Rimbaud running off to Africa
to look for gold and finding
an incurable case of syphilis;
Beethoven gone deaf;
Pound dragged through the streets
in a cage;
Chatterton taking rat poison;
Hemingway's brains dropping into
the orange juice;
Pascal cutting his wrists
in the bathtub;
Artaud locked up with the mad;
Dostoevsky stood up against a wall;
Crane jumping into a boat propeller
while in his pajamas;
Lorca shot in the road by Spanish
troops;
Berryman jumping off a bridge;
Burroughs shooting his wife;
Mailer knifing his.
—that's what they want:
a God damned show
a lit billboard
in the middle of hell.

that's what they want,
that bunch of
dull
inarticulate
safe
dreary
admirers of
carnivals.

one for the shoeshine man

the balance is in the snails climbing the
Santa Monica cliffs;
the luck is in walking down Western Avenue
and having one of the girls from a massage
parlor holler at you, "Hello, Sweetie!"
the miracle is in having five women in love
with you at the age of 55,
and the goodness is that you are only able
to love one of them.
the gift is in having a daughter more gentle
than you are, whose laughter is finer
than yours.
the placidity is in being able to drive a
blue 67 Volks through the streets like a
teenager, the radio on to The Host Who Loves You
Most, feeling the sun, feeling the solid hum
of the rebuilt motor
as you needle through traffic
pissing-off the dead.
the grace is in being able to like rock music,
symphony music, jazz . . .
anything that contains the joy of original
energy.
and the mathematic that returns
is the deep blue low
yourself flat upon yourself
within the guillotine walls—
angry at the sound of the phone
or anybody's footsteps passing;

and the other mathematic:
the imminent lilting high that follows
making the guys who sit on the benches
outside the taco stands
look like gurus
making the girl at the checkstand in the
supermarket look like
Marilyn
like Zsa Zsa
like Jackie before they got her Harvard lover
like the girl in high school that
all us boys followed home.

and the neatness which makes you believe
in something else besides death
is Sandy Hawley bringing in
five winners at Hollywood Park on off-form horses,
none of them favorites,
or somebody in a car approaching you
on a street too narrow,
and he or she pulls aside to let you
by, or the old fighter Beau Jack
shining shoes
after blowing the entire bankroll
on parties
on women
on parasites,
humming, blowing on the leather,
working the rag,

looking up and saying:
"what the hell, I had it for a
while, that beats the
other."

I act very bitter sometimes
but the taste has often been
sweet, it's only that I've
feared to say it. it's like
when your woman says,
"tell me you love me," and
you can't say it.

if you ever see me grinning from
my blue Volks
running a yellow light
driving straight into the sun
without dark shades
I will only be locked into the
afternoon of a
crazy life
thinking of trapeze artists
of midgets with big cigars
of a Russian winter in the early forties
of Chopin with his bag of Polish soil
or an old waitress bringing me an extra
cup of coffee and seeming to laugh at me
as she does so.

the best of you
I like more than you think.
the others don't count
except that they have fingers and heads
and some of them eyes
and most of them legs
and all of them
good and bad dreams
and a way to go.

the balance is everywhere and it's working
and the machineguns and the frogs
and the hedges will tell you
so.

the meek have inherited

if I suffer at this
typewriter
think how I'd feel
among the lettuce-
pickers
of Salinas?

I think of the men
I've known in
factories
with no way to
get out—
choking while living
choking while laughing
at Bob Hope or Lucille
Ball
while 2 or 3 children
beat tennis balls against
the walls.

some suicides are never
recorded.

who in the hell is Tom Jones?

I was shacked
with a 24 year old
girl from New York
City for two weeks,
along about the time
of the garbage strike
out there, and one night
this 34-year-old woman
arrived and she said,
"I want to see my rival,"
and she did and then
she said, "o, you're a
cute little thing!"
next I knew there was a
whirling of wildcats—
such screaming and scratching,
wounded animal moans,
blood and piss . . .

I was drunk and in my
shorts. I tried to
separate them and fell,
wrenched my knee. then
they were through the
door and down the walk
and out in the street.

squadcars full of cops
arrived. a police helicopter
circled overhead.

I stood in the bathroom
and grinned in the mirror.
it's not often at the
age of 55
that such splendid
action occurs.
it was better than the
Watts riots.

then the 34-year-old
came back in. she had pissed
all over herself and her
clothing was torn and
she was followed by 2 cops
who wanted to know
why.

pulling up my shorts
I tried to explain.

and a horse with greenblue eyes
walks on the sun

what you see is what you see:
madhouses are rarely
on display.

that we still walk about and
scratch ourselves and light
cigarettes

is more the miracle
than bathing beauties
than roses and the moth.

to sit in a small room
and drink a can of beer
and roll a cigarette
while listening to Brahms
on a small red radio

is to have come back
from a dozen wars
alive

listening to the sound
of the refrigerator

as the Pope hangs
the bathing beauties rot

and the oranges and apples
roll away.

an acceptance slip

16 years old
during the Depression
I'd come home drunk
and all my clothing—
shorts, shirts, stockings,
suitcase, and pages of
short stories
would be thrown on the
front lawn and about the
street.

my mother would be waiting
behind a tree:
"Henry, Henry, don't
go in . . . he'll
kill you, he's read
your stories . . ."

"I can whip his
ass . . ."

"Henry, please take
this . . . and
find yourself a room."

but it worried him
that I might not
finish high school

so I'd be back
again.

one evening he walked in
with the pages of
one of my short stories
(which I had never submitted
to him)
and he said, "this is
a great short story,"
and I said, "o.k.,"
and he handed it to me
and I read it.
it was a story about
a rich man
who had a fight with
his wife and had
gone out into the night
for a cup of coffee
and had noticed
the waitress and the spoons
and forks and the
salt and pepper shakers
and the neon sign
in the window
and then had gone back
to his stable
to see and touch his

favorite horse
who then
kicked him in the head
and killed him.

somehow
the story held
meaning for him
though
when I had written it
I had no idea
of what I was
writing about.

so I told him,
"o.k., old man, you can
have it."

and he took it
and walked out
and closed the door.
I guess that's
as close
as we ever got.

the end of a short affair

I tried it standing up
this time.
it usually doesn't
work
this time it seemed
to be . . .

she kept saying,
"oh my god, you've got
beautiful legs!"

it was all right
until she took her feet off the
ground
and wrapped her legs
around my center.

"oh my god, you've got
beautiful legs!"

she weighed about 138
pounds and hung there as I
worked.

it was when I climaxed
that I felt the pain
fly straight up my
spine.

I dropped her on the
couch and walked around
the room.
the pain remained.

"look," I told her,
"you'd better go. I've got
to develop some film
in my dark room."

she dressed and left
and I walked into the
kitchen for a glass of
water. I got a glass full
in my left hand.
the pain ran up behind my
ears and
I dropped the glass
which broke on the floor.

I got into a tub full of
hot water and Epsom salts.
I just got stretched out
when the phone rang.
as I tried to straighten
my back
the pain extended to my
neck and arms.
I flopped about,

gripped the sides of the tub,
got out
with shots of green and yellow
and red light
whirling in my head.

the phone kept ringing.
I picked it up.
"hello?"

"I LOVE YOU!" she said.

"thanks," I said.

"is that all you've got
to say?"

"yes."

"eat shit!" she said and
hung up.

love dries up, I thought
as I walked back to the
bathroom, about as fast as
sperm.

I made a mistake

I reached up into the top of the closet
and took out a pair of blue panties
and showed them to her and
asked "are these yours?"

and she looked and said,
"no, those belong to a dog."

she left after that and I haven't seen
her since. she's not at her place.
I keep going there, leaving notes stuck
into the door. I go back and the notes
are still there. I take the Maltese cross
cut it down from my car mirror, tie it
to her doorknob with a shoelace, leave
a book of poems.
when I go back the next night everything
is still there.

I keep searching the streets for that
blood-wine battleship she drives
with a weak battery, and the doors
hanging from broken hinges.

I drive around the streets
an inch away from weeping,
ashamed of my sentimentality and
possible love.

a confused old man driving in the rain
wondering where the good luck
went.

$$$$$

I've always had trouble with
money.
this one place I worked
everybody ate hot dogs
and potato chips
in the company cafeteria for
3 days before each
payday.
I wanted steaks,
I even went to see the manager
of the cafeteria and
demanded that he serve
steaks. he refused.

I'd forget payday.
I had a high rate of absenteeism and
payday would arrive and everybody would
start talking about
it.
"payday?" I'd say, "hell, is this
payday? I forgot to pick up my
last check . . ."

"stop the bullshit, man . . ."

"no, no, I mean it . . ."

I'd jump up and go down to payroll
and sure enough there'd be a
check and I'd come back and show it
to them. "Jesus Christ, I forgot all about
it . . ."

for some reason they'd get
angry. then the payroll clerk would come
around. I'd have two
checks. "Jesus," I'd say, "two checks."
and they were
angry.
some of them were working
two jobs.

the worst day
it was raining very hard,
I didn't have a raincoat so
I put on a very old coat I hadn't worn for
months and
I walked in a little late
while they were working.
I looked in the coat for some
cigarettes
and found a 5 dollar bill
in the side pocket:
"hey, look," I said, "I just found a 5 dollar

bill I didn't know I had, that's
funny."

"hey, man, knock off the
shit!"

"no, no, I'm *serious,* really, I remember
wearing this coat when
I got drunk at the
bars. I've been rolled too often,
I've got this fear . . . I take money out of
my wallet and hide it all
over me."

"sit down and get to
work."

I reached into an inside pocket:
"hey, look, here's a TWENTY! God, here's a
TWENTY I never knew I
had! I'm
RICH!"

"you're not funny, son of
a bitch . . ."

"hey, my God, here's ANOTHER
twenty! too much, too too

much . . . I *knew* I didn't spend all that
money that night. I thought I'd been
rolled again . . ."

I kept searching the
coat. "hey! here's a ten and
here's a fiver! my God . . ."

"listen, I'm telling you to *sit down
and shut up* . . ."

"my God, I'm RICH . . . I don't even *need*
this job . . ."

"man, sit *down* . . ."

I found another ten after I sat down
but I didn't say
anything.
I could feel waves of hatred and
I was confused,
they believed I had
plotted the whole thing
just to make them
feel bad. I didn't want
to. people who live on hot dogs and
potato chips for
3 days before payday

feel bad
enough.

I sat down
leaned forward and
began to go to
work.

outside
it continued to
rain.

metamorphosis

a girlfriend came in
built me a bed
scrubbed and waxed the kitchen floor
scrubbed the walls
vacuumed
cleaned the toilet
the bathtub
scrubbed the bathroom floor
and cut my toenails and
my hair.

then
all on the same day
the plumber came and fixed the kitchen faucet
and the toilet
and the gas man fixed the heater
and the phone man fixed the phone.
now I sit here in all this perfection.
it is quiet.
I have broken off with all 3 of my girlfriends.

I felt better when everything was in
disorder.
it will take me some months to get back to
normal:
I can't even find a roach to commune with.

I have lost my rhythm.
I can't sleep.
I can't eat.

I have been robbed of
my filth.

we've got to communicate

"he was a very sensitive man," she told me, "and after
he split with Andrea he kept her panties under his
pillow and each night he kissed them and cried.
look at you! look at that expression on your face!
you don't like what I just said and do you want to
know why?
it's because you're *afraid;* it takes a man to admit his feelings.
I see you watching women getting in and out of their
cars, hoping their skirts will climb up so you can
see their legs.
you're like a schoolboy, a peep-freak!
and *worse* than that, you just like to *think* about
sex, you really don't want to *do* it, it's only
work to you, you'd rather stare and imagine.
you don't even like to suck my breasts!
and you don't like to see a woman doing things in the
bathroom!
is there something *wrong* with bodily functions?
don't *you* have bodily functions?
Jesus, Christ, my sisters warned me about you!
they told me what you were like!
I didn't believe them, hell, you *looked* like a
man!
all your books, thousands of poems, and what do you
know?
you're afraid to look at a woman's pussy!
all you can do is *drink*!
do you think it takes any guts to drink?
here I've given you 5 years of my life and what do you

do?: you won't even *discuss* things with me!
you're charming enough when we have a party, that is,
if you're in the mood
you can really talk your shit
but look at you now, not a sound out of you, you just
sit in that chair over there and pour drink after
drink!
well, I've had it, I'm going to get myself somebody
real, somebody who can discuss things with me,
somebody who can say, 'well, look Paula, I realize
that we are having some problems and maybe
if we talk about them we can understand each other better
and make things work.'
not *you*! *look* at you! why don't you say something?
sure: DRINK IT DOWN! that's all you know how to do!
tell me, what's wrong with a woman's pussy?
my mother left my father because he was like you,
all he did was drink and play the horses!
well, he almost went crazy after she left him.
he pleaded and pleaded and pleaded for her to come
back, he even pretended he was dying of cancer just
to get her to come see him.
that didn't fool her—she went and got herself a decent
man, she's with him now, you've met him: Lance. but no,
you don't *like* Lance, do you?
he wears a necktie and he's into real estate . . .
well, he doesn't like you either. but mother loves him.
and what do *you* know about love?
it's a dirty word to you! *love*. you don't even 'like'!

you don't like your country, you don't like movies, you
don't like to dance, you don't like to drive on freeways,
you don't like children, you don't *look* at people,
all you do is sit in a chair and drink and figure systems
to beat the horses and if there's anything duller and
dumber than horses, you let me know, you just tell
me!
all you know how to do is to wake up sick each morning,
you can't get out of bed until noon; you drink whiskey,
you drink scotch, you drink beer, you drink wine, you
drink vodka, you drink gin, and what does it mean?
your health gets worse and worse, your left thumb is
dead, your liver is shot, you have high blood pressure,
hemorrhoids, ulcers and Christ knows what else,
and when I try to talk to you, you can't take it
and you run to your place and take the phone off
the hook and put on your symphony records and drink
yourself to sleep, and then you wake up sick at noon
and phone and say that you're dying and that you're
sorry and that you want to see me, and then I come over
and you're so *contrite* you're not even human—
oh, you can be *charming* when you're sick and in trouble,
you can be humorous, you can make me laugh, you win me back
again and again . . .
but look at you *now*! all you want is one more drink and then
one *more* drink and you won't talk to me, you just keep
lighting cigarettes and looking around the room . . .
don't you *want* to work at making our relationship better?
tell me, why are you afraid of a woman's pussy?"

the secret of my endurance

I still get letters in the mail, mostly from cracked-up
men in tiny rooms with factory jobs or no jobs who are
living with whores or no woman at all, no hope, just
booze and madness.
most of their letters are on lined paper
written with an unsharpened pencil
or in ink
in tiny handwriting that slants to the
left
and the paper is often torn
usually halfway up the middle
and they say they like my stuff,
I've written from where it's at, and
they recognize that. truly, I've given them a second
chance, some recognition of where they're at.

it's true, I was there, worse off than most
of them,
but I wonder if they realize where their letters
arrive?
well, they are dropped into a box
behind a six-foot hedge with a long driveway leading
to a two car garage, rose garden, fruit trees,
animals, a beautiful woman, mortgage about half
paid after a year, a new car,
fireplace and a green rug two-inches thick
with a young boy to write my stuff now,
I keep him in a ten-foot cage with a
typewriter, feed him whiskey and raw whores,

belt him pretty good three or four times
a week.
I'm 59 years old now and the critics say
my stuff is getting better than ever.

Carson McCullers

she died of alcoholism
wrapped in the blanket
of a deck chair
on an overseas
steamer

all her books of
terrified loneliness

all her books about
the cruelty
of the loveless lover

were all that were left
of her

as the strolling vacationer
discovered her body

notified the captain

and she was dispatched
somewhere else
upon the ship

as everything else
continued
as
she had written it.

sparks

the factory off Santa Fe Ave. was
best.
we packed heavy lighting fixtures into
long boxes
then flipped them up into stacks
six high.
then the loaders would
come by
clear your table and
you'd go for the next six.

ten hour day
four on Saturday
the pay was union
pretty good for unskilled labor
and if you didn't come in
with muscles
you got them soon enough

most of us in
white t-shirts and jeans
cigarettes dangling
sneaking beers
management looking
the other way

not many whites
the whites didn't last:
lousy workers

mostly Mexicans and
blacks
cool and mean

now and then
a blade flashed
or somebody got
punched-out

management looking
the other way

the few whites who lasted
were crazy

the work got done
and the young Mexican girls
kept us
cheerful and hoping
their eyes flashing
small messages
from the
assembly line.

I was one of the
crazy whites
who lasted
I was a good worker
just for the rhythm of it
just for the hell of it

and after ten hours
of heavy labor
after exchanging insults
living through skirmishes
with those not cool enough to
abide
we left
still fresh

we climbed into our old
automobiles to
go to our places
to drink half the night
to fight with our women

to return the next morning
to punch in
knowing we were
suckers
making the rich
richer

we swaggered
in our white t-shirts and
jeans
gliding past
the young Mexican girls

we were mean and perfect
for what we were

hungover
we could
very damn well
do the job

but
it didn't touch us
ever

those tin walls

the sound of drills and
cutting blades

the sparks

we were some gang
in that death ballet

we were magnificent

we gave them
better than they asked

yet

we gave them
nothing.

the history of a tough motherfucker

he came to the door one night wet boney beaten and
terrorized.
a white cross-eyed tailless cat
I took him in and fed him and he stayed
got to trust until a friend drove up the driveway
and ran him over
I took what was left to a vet who said, "not much
chance . . . give him these pills and wait . . . his backbone
is crushed, it was crushed once before but somehow
melded, if he lives he'll never walk again, look at
these x-rays, he's been shot, look here, the pellets
are still in him . . . also, he once had a tail, somebody
cut it off . . ."

I took the cat back, it was a hot summer, one of the
hottest summers in decades, I put him on the bathroom
floor, gave him water and pills, he wouldn't eat, he
wouldn't touch the water, I dipped my finger into it
and wet his mouth and I talked to him, I didn't go any-
where, I put in a lot of bathroom time and I talked to
him and gently touched him and he just looked back at
me with those pale blue crossed eyes as the days went
by he made his first move
dragging himself forward by his front legs
(the rear ones wouldn't move)
he made it to the litter box
crawled over and in,
that was like the horns of chance and possible victory
blowing away in the bathroom and into the city, I

related to that cat—I'd had it bad, not that kind of
bad but bad enough . . .

one morning he got up, stood up, fell back down and he
just looked at me.

"you make it, man," I said to him, "you're a good one . . ."

he kept trying it, getting up and falling down, finally
he walked a few steps, he was like a drunk weaving, the
rear legs just didn't want to do it and he fell again, rested,
then got up . . .

you know the rest: now he's better than ever, cross-eyed,
almost toothless, all the grace is back, and that look in
the eyes never left . . .

and now sometimes I'm interviewed, they want to hear about
life and literature and I get drunk and hold up my cross-eyed
shot runover de-tailed cat before them and I say, "look, look
at *this*!"

but they don't understand, they say something like, "you
say you've been influenced by Celine . . ."

"no," I hold the cat up before them, "by what happens, by
things like this, by this, by *this*! . . ."

I wobble the cat, holding him up under the front legs in
the smokey and drunken light; he's relaxed, he knows things . . .

it's about then that almost all the interviews end.
although I am very proud sometimes when I see the interviews
later and there I am and there is the cat and we are photo-
graphed together . . .

he knows it's bullshit too but it helps get the old cat food,
right?

oh, yes

there are worse things than
being alone
but it often takes decades
to realize this
and most often
when you do
it's too late
and there's nothing worse
than
too late.

retirement

pork chops, said my father, I love
pork chops!

and I watched him slide the grease
into his mouth.

pancakes, he said, pancakes with
syrup, butter and bacon!

I watched his lips heavy wetted with
all that.

coffee, he said, I like coffee so hot
it burns my throat!

sometimes it was too hot and he spit it
out across the table.

mashed potatoes and gravy, he said, I
love mashed potatoes and gravy!

he jowled that in, his cheeks puffed as
if he had the mumps.

chili and beans, he said, I love chili and
beans!

and he gulped it down and farted for hours
loudly, grinning after each fart.

strawberry shortcake, he said, with vanilla
ice-cream, that's the way to end a meal!

he always talked about retirement, about
what he was going to do when he
retired.
when he wasn't talking about food he talked
on and on about
retirement.

he never made it to retirement, he died one day while
standing at the sink
filling a glass of water.
he straightened like he'd been
shot.
the glass fell from his hand
and he dropped backwards
landing flat
his necktie slipping to the
left.

afterwards
people said they couldn't believe
it.
he looked
great.
distinguished white
sideburns, pack of smokes in his
shirt pocket, always cracking

jokes, maybe a little
loud and maybe with a bit of bad
temper
but all in all
a seemingly sound
individual

never missing a day
of work.

luck

once
we were young
at this
machine . . .
drinking
smoking
typing

it was a most
splendid
miraculous
time

still
is

only now
instead of
moving toward
time
it
moves toward
us

makes each word
drill
into the
paper

clear

fast

hard

feeding a
closing
space.

if you want justice, take the knife

undoubtedly we are alone
forever alone
and we
belong that way,
it was never meant
to be any other way—
I wouldn't want anybody waving fronds
over my ass
on a hot summer's night—
I'll take the heat
straight,
and when the time of death
arrives
the last thing I wish to see
is
a ring of human faces
about me—
better my old friends
the walls,
if they be there.

I have been alone but seldom
lonely.
I have partaken of the well
of myself
and the drinks were good,
the best I've had,
and tonight
sitting

staring into the darkness,
I know the darkness and the
light and the
in between.

and in spite of finding a
similarity between most
dung and most
people
I have been nearly content
with
the offerings.

the luck of the goodness
arrives
with accepting the
unwanted:
being born into this
fix—
the wasted gamble of our
joy,
the pleasure of
leaving—

cry not for me
but for tears

grieve not for me
but for grief

read
what I've written
then
forget it:

memory is a
trap: look to the walls
and begin
again.

cornered

well, they said it would come to
this: old. talent gone. fumbling for
the word

hearing the dark
footsteps, I turn
look behind me . . .

not yet, old dog . . .
soon enough.

now
they sit talking about
me: "yes, it's happened, he's
finished . . . it's
sad . . ."

"he never had a great deal, did
he?"

"well, no, but now . . ."

now
they are celebrating my demise
in taverns I no longer
frequent.

now
I drink alone

at this malfunctioning
machine

as the shadows assume
shapes
I fight the slow
retreat

now
my once-promise
dwindling
dwindling

now
lighting new cigarettes
pouring more
drinks

it has been a beautiful
fight

still
is.

how is your heart?

during my worst times
on the park benches
in the jails
or living with
whores
I always had this certain
contentment—
I wouldn't call it
happiness—
it was more of an inner
balance
that settled for
whatever was occurring
and it helped in the
factories
and when relationships
went wrong
with the
girls.

it helped
through the
wars and the
hangovers
the back alley fights
the
hospitals.

to awaken in a cheap room
in a strange city and
pull up the shade—
this was the craziest kind of
contentment
and to walk across the floor
to an old dresser with a
cracked mirror—
see myself, ugly,
grinning at it all.

what matters most is
how well you
walk through the
fire.

the burning of the dream

the old L.A. Public Library burned
down
that main library downtown
and with it went
a large part of my
youth.

I sat on one of those stone
benches there with my friend
Baldy when he
asked,
"you gonna join the
Abraham Lincoln
Brigade?"

"sure," I told
him.

but realizing that I wasn't
an intellectual or a political
idealist
I backed off on that
one.

I was a *reader*
then
going from room to
room: literature, philosophy,

religion, even medicine
and geology.

early on
I decided to be a writer,
I thought it might be the easy
way
out
and the big boy novelists didn't look
too tough to
me.
I had more trouble with
Hegel and Kant.

the thing that bothered
me
about everybody
is that they took too long
to finally say
something lively and/
or
interesting.
I thought I had it
over everybody
then.

I was to find two
things:

a) most publishers thought that anything
boring had something to do with things
profound.
b) that it would take decades of
living and writing
before I would be able to
put down
a sentence that was
anywhere near
what I wanted it to
be.

meanwhile
while other young men chased the
ladies
I chased the old
books.
I was a bibliophile, albeit a
disenchanted
one
and this
and the world
shaped me.

the old downtown library *was*
the place for me to be,
however—
at least during the days:

hungover and mal-
nourished.

I lived in a plywood hut
behind a roominghouse
for $3.50 a week
feeling like some Thomas
Chatterton
stuffed inside of some
Thomas Wolfe.

my greatest problem was
stamps, envelopes, paper
and
wine,
with the world on the edge
of World War II.
I hadn't yet been
confused by the
female, I was a virgin
and I wrote from 3 to
5 short stories a week
and they all came
back
from *The New Yorker, Harper's,*
The Atlantic Monthly.
I had read where
Ford Madox Ford used to paper

his bathroom with his
rejection slips
but I didn't have a
bathroom so I stuck them
into a drawer
until it got so fat with them
that I could barely
open it
so I took all the rejects out
and threw them
away along with the
stories.

still
the old L.A. Public Library was
my home
and the home of many other
bums.
we discreetly used the
restrooms and wiped our
bungholes
carefully
and the only ones of
us
to be evicted were those
who fell asleep at the
library
tables—nobody snores like a

bum
unless it's somebody you're married
to.

well, I wasn't *quite* a
bum. *I* had a library card
and I checked books in and
out
rapidly, large
stacks of them
always going the full
limit
allowed and I checked my
fellows in and
out:
Aldous Huxley, D. H. Lawrence,
e.e. cummings, Conrad Aiken, Fyodor
Dos, Dos Passos, Turgenev, Gorky,
H.D., Freddie Nietzsche, Art
Schopenhauer, Robert
Green,
Ingersoll, Steinbeck,
Hemingway,
and so
forth . . .

I always expected the librarian
to say, "nice taste there, young
man . . ."

but the old fried and wasted
bitch didn't even know who she
was
let alone
me.

but those walls had some
tremendous grace: they allowed
me to discover
the early Chinese poets
like Tu Fu and Li
Po
who could say more in one
line than most could say in
thirty or
ever.
Sherwood Anderson must have
read
these
too.

I also carried the *Cantos*
in and out
and Ezra helped me
strengthen my arms if not
my brain.

that place
the old L.A. Public Library

it was a home for a person who had had
a hell of a
home

BROOKS TOO BROAD FOR LEAPING
FAR FROM THE MADDING CROWD
POINT COUNTER POINT
THE HEART IS A LONELY HUNTER

James Thurber
John Fante
Rabelais
de Maupassant

some didn't work for
me: Shakespeare, G. B. Shaw,
Tolstoy, Robert Frost, F. Scott
Fitzgerald

Upton Sinclair worked better for
me
than Sinclair Lewis
and I considered Gogol and
Dreiser complete
flops.

but such judgments happen more
from a man's inbred and/or

forced manner of living than from
his
reason.

the old L.A. Public
most probably kept me from
becoming a
suicide
a bank
robber
a
wife-
beater
a butcher or a
motorcycle policeman
and even though some of these
might have some fine
qualities
it is
I think
thanks
to my luck
and my way
that this library was
there when I was
young and looking to
hold on to
something

when there seemed very
little
about.

and when I opened the
newspaper
and read of the fire
which almost
destroyed the entire
library and most of
its contents

I said to my
wife: "I used to hang
out
there . . ."

THE PRUSSIAN OFFICER
THE DARING YOUNG MAN ON THE FLYING TRAPEZE
TO HAVE AND HAVE NOT

YOU CAN'T GO HOME AGAIN.

hell is a lonely place

he was 65, his wife was 66, had
Alzheimer's disease.

he had cancer of the
mouth.
there were
operations, radiation
treatments
which decayed the bones in his
jaw
which then had to be
wired.

daily he put his wife in
rubber diapers
like a
baby.

unable to drive in his
condition
he had to take a taxi to
the medical
center,
had difficulty speaking,
had to
write the directions
down.

on his last visit
they informed him
there would be another
operation: a bit more
of the inner left
cheek and a bit more
of
the tongue.

when he returned
he changed his wife's
diapers
put on the tv
dinners, watched the
evening news
then went to the
bedroom, got the
gun, put it to her
temple, fired.

she fell to the
left, he sat upon the
couch
put the gun into his
mouth, pulled the
trigger
the shots didn't arouse
the neighbors.

later
the burning tv dinners
did.

somebody arrived, pushed
the door open, saw
it.

soon
the police arrived and
went through their
routine, found
some items:

a closed savings
account and
a checkbook with a
balance of
$1.14

suicide, they
deduced.

in three weeks
there were two
new tenants:
a computer engineer
named

Ross
and his wife
Anatana
who studied
ballet.

they looked like another
upwardly mobile
pair.

the strongest of the strange

you won't see them often
for wherever the crowd is
they
are not.

these odd ones, not
many
but from them
come
the few
good paintings
the few
good symphonies
the few
good books
and other
works.

and from the
best of the
strange ones
perhaps
nothing.

they are
their own
paintings
their own

books
their own
music
their own
work.

sometimes I think
I see
them—say
a certain old
man
sitting on a
certain bench
in a certain
way

or
a quick face
going the other
way
in a passing
automobile

or
there's a certain motion
of the hands
of a bag-boy or a bag-
girl

while packing
supermarket
groceries.

sometimes
it is even somebody
you have been
living with
for some
time—
you will notice
a
lightning quick
glance
never seen
from them
before.

sometimes
you will only note
their
presence
suddenly
in quite
vivid
recall
some months
some years

after they are
gone.

I remember
such a
one—
he was about
20 years old
drunk at
10 a.m.
staring into
a cracked
New Orleans
mirror

face dreaming
against the
walls of
the world

where
did I
go?

8 count

from my bed
I watch
3 birds
on a telephone
wire.

one flies
off.
then
another.

one is left,
then
it too
is gone.

my typewriter is
tombstone
still.

and I am
reduced to bird
watching.

just thought I'd
let you
know,
fucker.

we ain't got no money, honey, but we got rain

call it the greenhouse effect or whatever
but it just doesn't rain like it
used to.

I particularly remember the rains of the
depression era.
there wasn't any money but there was
plenty of rain.

it wouldn't rain for just a night or
a day,
it would RAIN for 7 days and 7
nights
and in Los Angeles the storm drains
weren't built to carry off that much
water
and the rain came down THICK and
MEAN and
STEADY
and you HEARD it banging against
the roofs and into the ground
waterfalls of it came down
from the roofs
and often there was HAIL
big ROCKS OF ICE
bombing
exploding
smashing into things
and the rain
just wouldn't

STOP
and all the roofs leaked—
dishpans,
cooking pots
were placed all about;
they dripped loudly
and had to be emptied
again and
again

the rain came up over the street curbings,
across the lawns, climbed the steps and
entered the houses.
there were mops and bathroom towels,
and the rain often came up through the
toilets: bubbling, brown, crazy, whirling,
and the old cars stood in the streets,
cars that had problems starting on a
sunny day,
and the jobless men stood
looking out the windows
at the old machines dying
like living things
out there.

the jobless men,
failures in a failing time
were imprisoned in their houses with their
wives and children
and their

pets.
the pets refused to go out
and left their waste in
strange places.

the jobless men went mad
confined with
their once beautiful wives.
there were terrible arguments
as notices of foreclosure
fell into the mailbox.
rain and hail, cans of beans,
bread without butter; fried
eggs, boiled eggs, poached
eggs; peanut butter
sandwiches, and an invisible
chicken
in every pot.

my father, never a good man
at best, beat my mother
when it rained
as I threw myself
between them,
the legs, the knees, the
screams
until they
separated.

"*I'll kill you,*" I screamed
at him. "*You hit her again
and I'll kill you!*"

"*Get that son-of-a-bitching
kid out of here!*"

"no, Henry, you stay with
your mother!"

all the households were under
siege but I believe that ours
held more terror than the
average.

and at night
as we attempted to sleep
the rains still came down
and it was in bed
in the dark
watching the moon against
the scarred window
so bravely
holding out
most of the rain,
I thought of Noah and the
Ark
and I thought, it has come
again.

we all thought
that.

and then, at once, it would
stop.
and it always seemed to
stop
around 5 or 6 a.m.,
peaceful then,
but not an exact silence
because things continued to
drip
drip
drip

and there was no smog then
and by 8 a.m.
there was a
blazing yellow sunlight,
Van Gogh yellow—
crazy, blinding!
and then
the roof drains
relieved of the rush of
water
began to expand in
the warmth:
PANG! PANG! PANG!

and everybody got up
and looked outside
and there were all the lawns
still soaked
greener than green will ever
be
and there were the birds
on the lawn
CHIRPING like mad,
they hadn't eaten decently
for 7 days and 7 nights
and they were weary of
berries
and
they waited as the worms
rose to the top,
half-drowned worms.
the birds plucked them
up
and gobbled them
down; there were
blackbirds and sparrows.
the blackbirds tried to
drive the sparrows off
but the sparrows,
maddened with hunger,
smaller and quicker,
got their
due.

the men stood on their porches
smoking cigarettes,
now knowing
they'd have to go out
there
to look for that job
that probably wasn't
there, to start that car
that probably wouldn't
start.

and the once beautiful
wives
stood in their bathrooms
combing their hair,
applying makeup,
trying to put their world back
together again,
trying to forget that
awful sadness that
gripped them,
wondering what they could
fix for
breakfast.

and on the radio
we were told that
school was now
open.

and
soon
there I was
on the way to school,
massive puddles in the
street,
the sun like a new
world,
my parents back in that
house,
I arrived at my classroom
on time.

Mrs. Sorenson greeted us
with, "we won't have our
usual recess, the grounds
are too wet."

"AW!" most of the boys
went.

"but we are going to do
something special at
recess," she went on,
"and it will be
fun!"

well, we all wondered
what that would

be
and the two hour wait
seemed a long time
as Mrs. Sorenson
went about
teaching her
lessons.

I looked at the little
girls, they all looked so
pretty and clean and
alert,
they sat still and
straight
and their hair was
beautiful
in the California
sunshine.

then the recess bell rang
and we all waited for the
fun.

then Mrs. Sorenson told
us:
"now, what we are going to
do is we are going to tell
each other what we did
during the rainstorm!
we'll begin in the front

row and go right around!
now, Michael, you're
first! . . ."

well, we all began to tell
our stories, Michael began
and it went on and on,
and soon we realized that
we were all lying, not
exactly lying but mostly
lying and some of the boys
began to snicker and some
of the girls began to give
them dirty looks and
Mrs. Sorenson said,
"all right, I demand a
modicum of silence
here!
I am interested in what
you did
during the rainstorm
even if you
aren't!"

so we had to tell our
stories and they *were*
stories.

one girl said that
when the rainbow first

came
she saw God's face
at the end of it.
only she didn't say
which end.

one boy said he stuck
his fishing pole
out the window
and caught a little
fish
and fed it to his
cat.

almost everybody told
a lie.
the truth was just
too awful and
embarrassing to
tell.

then the bell rang
and recess was
over.

"thank you," said Mrs.
Sorenson, "that was very
nice
and tomorrow the grounds
will be dry

and we will put them
to use
again."

most of the boys
cheered
and the little girls
sat very straight and
still,
looking so pretty and
clean and
alert,
their hair beautiful
in a sunshine that
the world might
never see
again.

flophouse

you haven't lived
until you've been in a
flophouse
with nothing but one
light bulb
and 56 men
squeezed together
on cots
with everybody
snoring
at once
and some of those
snores
so
deep and
gross and
unbelievable—
dark
snotty
gross
subhuman
wheezings
from hell
itself.

your mind
almost breaks
under that

sound

and the
intermingling
stinks:
hard
unwashed socks
pissed and
shitted
underwear

and over it all
slowly circulating
air
much like that
emanating from
uncovered
garbage
cans.

and those
bodies
in the dark

fat and
thin
and
twisted

some
legless
armless

some
mindless

and worst of
all:
the total
absence of
hope

it shrouds
them
covers them
totally.

it's not
worth
it.

you get
up

go out

walk the
streets

up and
down
sidewalks

past buildings

around the
corner

and back
up
the same
street

thinking

these men
were all
children
once

what
has
happened
to
them?

and what
has

happened
to
me?

it's dark
and cold
out
here.

the soldier, his wife and the bum

I was a bum in San Francisco but once managed
to go to a symphony concert along with the well-dressed
people
and the music was good but something about the
audience was not
and something about the orchestra
and the conductor was
not,
although the building was fine and the
acoustics perfect
I preferred to listen to the music alone
on my radio
and afterwards I did go back to my room and I
turned on the radio but
then there was a pounding on the wall:
"SHUT THAT GOD-DAMNED THING OFF!"

there was a soldier in the next room
living with his wife
and he would soon be going over there to protect
me from Hitler so
I snapped the radio off and then heard his
wife say, "you shouldn't have done that."
and the soldier said, "FUCK THAT GUY!"
which I thought was a very nice thing for him
to tell his wife to do.
of course,
she never did.

anyhow, I never went to another live concert
and I always listened to the radio very
quietly, my ear pressed to the
speaker.

war has its price and millions of young men
everywhere would die
and as I listened to the classical music I
heard them making love, desperately and
mournfully, through Shostakovich, Brahms,
Mozart, through crescendo and climax,
and through the shared
wall of our
darkness.

no leaders

invent yourself and then reinvent yourself,
don't slough in the slime.
invent yourself and then reinvent yourself,
stay out of the clutches of mediocrity and
self-pity.

invent yourself and then reinvent yourself,
change your tone and shape so that they can
never
find you.

recharge yourself.
accept continuance
but only on the terms that you have invented
and reinvented.

be self-instructed.

invent life,
it is you,
the history of its past and
the presence of its presentness.
there is nothing else,
nothing.

Dinosauria, we

born like this
into this
as the chalk faces smile
as Mrs. Death laughs
as the elevators break
as political landscapes dissolve
as the supermarket bag boy holds a college degree
as the oily fish spit out their oily prey
as the sun is masked

we are
born like this
into this
into these carefully mad wars
into the sight of broken factory windows of emptiness
into bars where people no longer speak to each other
into fist fights that end as shootings and knifings

born into this
into hospitals which are so expensive that it's cheaper to die
into lawyers who charge so much it's cheaper to plead guilty
into a country where the jails are full and the madhouses closed
into a place where the masses elevate fools into rich heroes

born into this
walking and living through this
dying because of this
muted because of this
castrated
debauched

disinherited
because of this
fooled by this
used by this
pissed on by this
made crazy and sick by this
made violent
made inhuman
by this

the heart is blackened
the fingers reach for the throat
the gun
the knife
the bomb
the fingers reach toward an unresponsive god

the fingers reach for the bottle
the pill
the powder

we are born into this sorrowful deadliness
we are born into a government 60 years in debt
that soon will be unable to even pay the interest on that debt
and the banks will burn
money will be useless
there will be open and unpunished murder in the streets
it will be guns and roving mobs
land will be useless
food will become a diminishing return

nuclear power will be taken over by the many
explosions will continually shake the earth
radiated robot men will stalk each other
the rich and the chosen will watch from space platforms
Dante's Inferno will be made to look like a children's playground

the sun will not be seen and it will always be night
trees will die
all vegetation will die
radiated men will eat the flesh of radiated men
the sea will be poisoned
the lakes and rivers will vanish
rain will be the new gold

the rotting bodies of men and animals will stink in the dark wind

the last few survivors will be overtaken by new and hideous
diseases
and the space platforms will be destroyed by attrition
the petering out of supplies
the natural effect of general decay

and there will be the most beautiful silence never heard

born out of that.

the sun still hidden there

awaiting the next chapter.

nirvana

not much chance,
completely cut loose from
purpose,
he was a young man
riding a bus
through North Carolina
on the way to
somewhere
and it began to snow
and the bus stopped
at a little cafe
in the hills
and the passengers
entered.

he sat at the counter
with the others,
he ordered and the
food arrived.
the meal was
particularly
good
and the
coffee.

the waitress was
unlike the women
he had
known.
she was unaffected,

there was a natural
humor which came
from her.
the fry cook said
crazy things.
the dishwasher,
in back,
laughed, a good
clean
pleasant
laugh.

the young man watched
the snow through the
windows.

he wanted to stay
in that cafe
forever.

the curious feeling
swam through him
that everything
was
beautiful
there,
that it would always
stay beautiful
there.

then the bus driver
told the passengers
that it was time
to board.

the young man
thought, I'll just sit
here, I'll just stay
here.

but then
he rose and followed
the others into the
bus.

he found his seat
and looked at the cafe
through the bus
window.

then the bus moved
off, down a curve,
downward, out of
the hills.

the young man
looked straight
forward.
he heard the other
passengers

speaking
of other things,
or they were
reading
or
attempting to
sleep.

they had not
noticed
the
magic.

the young man
put his head to
one side,
closed his
eyes,
pretended to
sleep.
there was nothing
else to do—
just listen to the
sound of the
engine,
the sound of the
tires
in the
snow.

the bluebird

there's a bluebird in my heart that
wants to get out
but I'm too tough for him,
I say, stay in there, I'm not going
to let anybody see
you.

there's a bluebird in my heart that
wants to get out
but I pour whiskey on him and inhale
cigarette smoke
and the whores and the bartenders
and the grocery clerks
never know that
he's
in there.

there's a bluebird in my heart that
wants to get out
but I'm too tough for him,
I say,
stay down, do you want to mess
me up?
you want to screw up the
works?
you want to blow my book sales in
Europe?

there's a bluebird in my heart that

wants to get out
but I'm too clever, I only let him out
at night sometimes
when everybody's asleep.
I say, I know that you're there,
so don't be
sad.

then I put him back,
but he's singing a little
in there, I haven't quite let him
die
and we sleep together like
that
with our
secret pact
and it's nice enough to
make a man
weep, but I don't
weep, do
you?

the secret

don't worry, nobody has the
beautiful lady, not really, and
nobody has the strange and
hidden power, nobody is
exceptional or wonderful or
magic, they only seem to be.
it's all a trick, an in, a con,
don't buy it, don't believe it.
the world is packed with
billions of people whose lives
and deaths are useless and
when one of these jumps up
and the light of history shines
upon them, forget it, it's not
what it seems, it's just
another act to fool the fools
again.

there are no strong men, there
are no beautiful women.
at least, you can die knowing
this
and you will have
the only possible
victory.

fan letter

I been readin' you for a long time now,
I just put Billy Boy to bed,
he got 7 mean ticks from somewhere,
I got 2,
my husband, Benny, he got 3.
some of us love bugs, others hate
them.
Benny writes poems.
he was in the same magazine as you
once.
Benny is the world's greatest writer
but he got this temper.
he gave a reading once and somebody
laughed at one of his serious poems
and Benny took his thing out right
there
and pissed on stage.
he says you write good but that you
couldn't carry his balls in a paper
bag.
anyhow, I made a BIG POT OF MARMALADE
tonight,
we all just LOVE marmalade here.
Benny lost his job yesterday, he told his
boss to stick it up his ass
but I still got my job down at the
manicure shop.
you know fags come in to get their nails
done?

you aren't a fag, are you, Mr.
Chinaski?
anyhow, I just felt like writing you.
your books are read and read around
here.
Benny says you're an old fart, you
write pretty good but that you
couldn't carry his balls in a
paper sack.
do you like bugs, Mr. Chinaski?
I think the marmalade is cool enough to
eat now.
so goodbye.
     Dora

to lean back into it

like in a chair the color of the sun
as you listen to lazy piano music
and the aircraft overhead are not
for war.
where the last drink is as good as
the first
and you realize that the promises
you made yourself were
kept.
that's plenty.
that last: about the promises.
what's not so good is that the few
friends you had are
dead and they seem
irreplaceable.
on women, you didn't know enough
early
and too much
too late.
and if self-analysis is allowed:
nice that you turned out well-
honed,
that you arrived late
and remain generally
capable.
outside of that, not much.
except you can leave without
regret.
until then, a bit more play,

a bit more endurance,
leaning back into it,
like the dog who got across
the busy street:
not all of it was good
luck.

do you want to enter the arena?

if it doesn't come rushing out of you,
don't do it.
unless it comes bursting out of your
ears and your head and your ass
and your bellybutton,
don't do it.
if you have to sit for an hour
staring at your computer screen
or hunched over your
typewriter,
don't do it.
if you're doing it for money or
fame,
don't do it.
if you're doing it because you want
women in your bed,
don't do it.
if you have to sit there and
rework it, rewrite it,
don't do it.
if it's hard work doing it,
don't do it.
if you're trying to write like somebody
else,
don't do it.

if you have to wait for it to roar out of
you,

then wait.
if it never roars out of you,
do something else.

if you have to read it to your wife
or your girlfriend or your boyfriend
or your parents or anybody at all,
you're not ready.

don't be like so many writers,
don't be so like so many thousands of
writers who call themselves writers,
don't be so dull and boring and
pretentious, don't lock in with self-
love.
don't work the pages to death with
your crap.
the libraries of the world have
yawned themselves to
sleep.
don't add to that,
don't do it.
unless it comes bursting through
your skull like a rocket,
unless being still about it would
drive you to madness or
suicide or murder,
don't do it.

unless the sun inside of you is
burning your guts out,
don't do it.

when it is known to you truly,
it will do it by
itself and it will keep doing it
until you die or it dies in
you.

there is no other way.

there never was.

the condition book

the long days at the track have indented themselves
into me:
I am the horses, the jocks, I am six furlongs, seven
furlongs, I am a mile and one sixteenth, I am a
handicap, I am all the colors of all the silks, I am all
the photo finishes, the accidents, the deaths, the
last place finishers, the breakdowns, the failure of
the toteboard, the dropped whip and the numb pain
of the dream not come true in thousands and thousands
and thousands of faces, I am the long drive home in the
dark, in the rain, I am decades and decades and decades
of races run and won and lost and run again and I am
myself sitting with a program and a *Racing Form.*
I am the racetrack, my ribs are the wooden rails, my
eyes are the flashes of the toteboard, my feet are
hooves and there is something riding on my back, I am
the last curve, I am the home stretch, I am the longshot
and the favorite, I am the exacta, the daily double and
the pick 6.
I am humanely destroyed, I am the horseplayer who
became the
racetrack.

a new war

a different fight now, warding off the weariness of
old age,
retreating to your room, stretching out upon the bed,
there's not much will to move,
it's near midnight now.

not so long ago your night would be just
beginning, but don't lament lost youth:
youth was no wonder
either.

but now it's the waiting on death.
it's not death that's the problem, it's the waiting.

you should have been dead decades ago.
the abuse you loaded upon yourself was
enormous and non-ending.
a different fight now, yes, but nothing to
mourn about, only to
note.

frankly, it's even a bit dull waiting on the
blade.

and to think, after I'm gone,
there will be more for others, other days,
other nights.
dogs walking sidewalks, trees shaking in
the wind.

I won't be leaving much.
something to read, maybe.

a wild onion in the gutted
road.

Paris in the dark.

the laughing heart

your life is your life.
don't let it be clubbed into dank
submission.
be on the watch.
there are ways out.
there is light somewhere.
it may not be much light but
it beats the
darkness.
be on the watch.
the gods will offer you
chances.
know them, take them.
you can't beat death but
you can beat death
in life,
sometimes.
and the more often you
learn to do it,
the more light there will
be.
your life is your life.
know it while you have
it.
you are marvelous
the gods wait to delight
in
you.

roll the dice

if you're going to try, go all the
way.
otherwise, don't get into it.

if you're going to try, go all the
way.
this could mean losing girlfriends,
wives, relatives, jobs and
maybe your mind.

go all the way.
it could mean not eating for 3 or
4 days.
it could mean freezing on a
park bench.
it could mean jail, alcoholism,
it could mean derision,
mockery,
isolation.
isolation is the gift,
all the other is a test of your
guts,
of how much you really want to
do it.
and you'll do it
against total rejection and the
highest of odds
and it will be better than

anything else
you can think of.

if you're going to try,
go all the way.
there is no other feeling like
it.
you will be alone with the
gods
and the nights will flame with
fire.

do it, do it, do it.
do it.

all the way
all the way.

you will ride death straight to
hell,
your perfect laughter,
the only good fight
now.

so now?

the words have come and gone,
I sit ill.
the phone rings, the cats sleep.
Linda vacuums.
I am waiting to live,
waiting to die.

I wish I could ring in some bravery.
it's a lousy fix
but the tree outside doesn't know:
I watch it moving with the wind
in the late afternoon sun.

there's nothing to declare here,
just a waiting.
each faces it alone.

Oh, I was once young,
Oh, I was once unbelievably
young!

the crunch

too much
too little

too fat
too thin
or nobody.

laughter or
tears

haters
lovers

strangers with faces like
the backs of
thumbtacks
armies running through
streets of blood
waving winebottles
bayoneting and fucking
virgins.

or an old guy in a cheap room
with a photograph of M. Monroe.

there is a loneliness in this world so great
that you can see it in the slow movement of
the hands of a clock.

people so tired
mutilated
either by love or no love.

people just are not good to each other
one on one.

the rich are not good to the rich
the poor are not good to the poor.

we are afraid.

our educational system tells us
that we can all be
big-ass winners.

it hasn't told us
about the gutters
or the suicides.

or the terror of one person
aching in one place
alone

untouched
unspoken to

watering a plant.

people are not good to each other.
people are not good to each other.
people are not good to each other.

I suppose they never will be.
I don't ask them to be.

but sometimes I think about
it.

the beads will swing
the clouds will cloud
and the killer will behead the child
like taking a bite out of an ice-cream cone.

too much
too little
too fat
too thin
or nobody

more haters than lovers.

people are not good to each other.
perhaps if they were
our deaths would not be so sad.

meanwhile I look at young girls
stems

flowers of chance.

there must be a way.

surely there must be a way we have not yet
thought of.

who put this brain inside of me?

it cries
it demands
it says that there is a chance.

it will not say
"no."

SOURCES

"friendly advice to a lot of young men, and a lot of old men, too." (c. 1954); *Existaria* 7, September-October 1957; collected in *The Roominghouse Madrigals*, 1988.

"as the sparrow." *Quixote* 13, Spring 1957; collected in *The Days Run Away Like Wild Horses Over the Hills*, 1969.

"layover." *The Naked Ear* 9, late 1957; collected in *The Roominghouse . . .*

"the life of Borodin." *Quicksilver* 11.3, Autumn 1958; collected in *Burning in Water, Drowning in Flame*, 1974.

"when Hugo Wolf went mad." *Odyssey* 5, 1959; collected in *The Days . . .*

"destroying beauty." (Early 1959); *The Roominghouse . . .*

"the day I kicked a bankroll out the window." *Quicksilver* 12.2, Summer 1959; collected in *The Roominghouse . . .*

"the twins." *Galley Sail Review* 1.4, Autumn 1959; collected in *Burning . . .*

"to the whore who took my poems." *Quagga* 1.3, September 1960; collected in *Burning . . .*

"the loser." *The Sparrow* 14, November 1960; collected in *The Roominghouse . . .*

"the best way to get famous is to run away." (Late 1960); *Longshot Pomes for Broken Players*, September 1961; collected in *The Roominghouse* . . .

"the tragedy of the leaves." *Targets* 4, December 1960; collected in *Burning* . . .

"old man, dead in a room." *The Outsider* 1, Fall 1961; collected in *The Roominghouse* . . .

"the priest and the matador." *Epos* 13.2, Winter 1961; collected in *Burning* . . .

"the state of world affairs from a 3rd floor window." *Rongwrong* 1, 1961; collected in *Burning* . . .

"the swan." (c. 1961); *Notes from Underground* 1, 1964; collected in *The Days* . . .

"beans with garlic." April 1, 1962 manuscript; collected in *Burning* . . .

"a poem is a city." *Targets* 10, June 1962; collected in *The Days* . . .

"consummation of grief." *Sun* 8, 1962; collected in *Mockingbird Wish Me Luck*, 1972.

"for Jane: with all the love I had, which was not enough." 1962 manuscript; collected in *The Days* . . .

"for Jane." *The Wormwood Review* 8, December 1962; collected in *The Days* . . .

"john dillinger and *le chasseur maudit*." (c. 1963–64); *Burning* . . .

"crucifix in a deathhand." collected in *Burning* . . .

"something for the touts, the nuns, the grocery clerks and you . . ." *crucifix in a deathhand,* 1965; collected in *Burning* . . .

"no. 6." *crucifix in a deathhand,* 1965; collected in *Burning* . . .

"and the moon and the stars and the world:" 1965 manuscript; collected in *The Days* . . .

"true story." *true story* broadside, April 1966; collected in *Burning* . . .

"the genius of the crowd." *the genius of the crowd* chapbook, June 1966; collected in *The Roominghouse* . . .

"I met a genius." *the flower lover—I met a genius* broadside, October 1966; collected in *Burning* . . .

"swastika star buttoned to my ass." *Iconolatre* 18/19, 1966; previously uncollected.

"the blackbirds are rough today." (c. 1966–67); *The Roominghouse* . . .

"if we take—" *if we take*—New Year's Greeting, December 1969; collected in *Mockingbird* . . .

"another academy." *Wormwood Review* 38, Spring 1970; collected in *Mockingbird* . . .

"the poetry reading." *California Librarian* 31.4, October 1970; collected in *Mockingbird* . . .

"the last days of the suicide kid." *Invisible City* 1, February 1971; collected in *Mockingbird* . . .

"the shower." March 1971 manuscript; collected in *Mockingbird* . . .

"style." March 1971 manuscript; collected in *Mockingbird* . . .

"the mockingbird." April 1971 manuscript; collected in *Mockingbird* . . .

"girl in a miniskirt reading the Bible outside my window." *Mano Mano* 2, July 1971; collected in *Mockingbird* . . .

"the shoelace." *Vagabond* 11, 1971; collected in *Mockingbird* . . .

"those sons of bitches." *Cotyledon* 2, Spring 1972; collected in *Mockingbird* . . .

"hot." *Event* 2.2, 1972; collected in *Burning* . . .

"trouble with Spain." *Stonecloud* 2, 1973; collected in *Burning* . . .

"a radio with guts." *Stonecloud* 2, 1973; collected in *Play the Piano Drunk Like a Percussion Instrument Until the Fingers Begin to Bleed a Bit*, 1979.

"love poem to Marina." *Second Coming* 2.3, 1973; collected in *On Love*, 2016.

"some people never go crazy." *Two Charlies* 3, 1973; collected as "some people" in *Burning* . . .

"the fisherman." *Burning* . . .

"the trash men." *Burning* . . .

"face of a political candidate on a street billboard." May 14, 1974 manuscript; collected in *Play the Piano* . . .

"the proud thin dying." July 21, 1974 manuscript; collected in *Play the Piano* . . .

"an almost made up poem." *Aunt Harriet's Flair for Writing Review* 1, 1974; collected in *Love Is a Dog from Hell*, 1977.

"a love poem for all the women I have known." September 15, 1974 manuscript (second draft); collected as "a love poem" in *War All the Time*, 1984.

"art." December 24, 1974 manuscript; collected in *Play the Piano* . . .

"what they want." February 27, 1975 manuscript; collected in *Love Is a Dog* . . .

"one for the shoeshine man." May 17, 1975 manuscript; collected in *Love Is a Dog* . . .

"the meek have inherited." June 4, 1975 manuscript; collected in *Love Is a Dog* . . .

"who in the hell is Tom Jones?" June 4, 1975 manuscript; collected in *Love Is a Dog* . . .

"and a horse with greenblue eyes walks on the sun." June 22, 1975 manuscript; collected in *Love Is a Dog* . . .

"an acceptance slip." November 27, 1975 manuscript; collected in *Love Is a Dog* . . . as "my old man," and as "acceptance" in *The People Look Like Flowers at Last*, 2007.

"the end of a short affair." January 19, 1976 manuscript; collected in *Love Is a Dog* . . .

"I made a mistake." *Scarlet*, April 1976; collected in *Love Is a Dog* . . .

"$$$$$$." *Love Is a Dog* . . .

"metamorphosis." *Play the Piano . . .*

"we've got to communicate." July 22, 1979 manuscript; collected in *Dangling in the Tournefortia*, 1981.

"the secret of my endurance." October 4, 1979 manuscript; collected in *Dangling . . .*

"Carson McCullers." October 24, 1981 manuscript; collected in *The Night Torn Mad with Footsteps*, 2001.

"sparks." February 9, 1982 manuscript; collected in *War All the Time.*

"the history of a tough motherfucker." February 28, 1983, manuscript (second draft); collected in *War All the Time.*

"oh, yes." April 11, 1983 manuscript; collected in *War All the Time.*

"retirement." November 1984 manuscript; collected as "retired" in *You Get So Alone at Times That It Just Makes Sense*, 1986.

"luck." April 1985 manuscript; collected in *Septuagenarian Stew*, 1990.

"if you want justice, take the knife." September 14, 1985 manuscript; collected as "mind and heart" in *Come On In!*, 2006.

"cornered." *cornered* chapbook, October 1985; collected in *You Get So Alone . . .*

"how is your heart?" 1985 manuscript; collected in *You Get So Alone . . .*

"the burning of the dream." Spring 1986 manuscript; collected in *Septuagenarian . . .*

"hell is a lonely place." (c. 1987); *Synaesthesia* 2, 1989; collected in *Septuagenarian* . . .

"the strongest of the strange." *Scream Magazine* 6, 1989; collected in *Septuagenarian* . . .

"8 count." c. 1989 manuscript; collected in *The Last Night of the Earth Poems,* 1992.

"we ain't got no money, honey, but we got rain." *we ain't got no money, honey, but we got rain* New Year's Greeting, 1990; collected in *The Last Night* . . .

"flophouse." (c. 1990); *Wormwood Review* 141, 1996; collected in *The Last Night* . . .

"the soldier, his wife and the bum." (c. 1990); *Wormwood Review* 142, 1996; collected in *The Last Night* . . .

"no leaders." c. 1990 manuscript; collected as "no leaders, please" in *Come On In!*

"Dinosauria, we." February 13, 1991 manuscript; collected in *The Last Night* . . .

"nirvana." February 24, 1991 manuscript; collected in *The Last Night* . . .

"the bluebird." *the bluebird* broadside, September 1991; collected in *The Last Night* . . .

"the secret." *Painted Bride Quarterly* 43, 1991; collected in *Betting on the Muse,* 1996.

"fan letter." *The Last Night* . . .

"to lean back into it." *Red Tree* 4, Summer 1992; collected in

What Matters Most Is How Well You Walk Through the Fire, 1999.

"do you want to enter the arena?" October 20, 1992 manuscript; collected as "so you want to be a writer?" in *Sifting Through the Madness for the Word, the Line, the Way*, 2003.

"the condition book." November 10, 1992 manuscript; collected in *The Night Torn . . .*

"a new war." (c. 1992); *Prairie Schooner* 67.3, Fall 1993; collected in *What Matters Most . . .*

"the laughing heart." (c. 1992); *Prairie Schooner* 67.3, Fall 1993; collected in *Betting . . .*

"roll the dice." c. 1993 manuscript; collected in *What Matters Most . . .*

"so now?" Early 1994 manuscript; collected in *Betting . . .*

"the crunch." September 13, 1976 manuscript (second draft); collected in *Love Is a Dog . . .*

ACKNOWLEDGMENTS

The editor and publisher would like to thank the owners of the poems here printed, which include the following institutions:

University of Arizona, Special Collections

The University of California, Los Angeles, Special Collections

The University of California, Santa Barbara, Special Collections

The Huntington Library, San Marino, California

Indiana University, Lilly Library

The University of Southern California, Rare Books Collection

Thanks also to the following magazines, where some of the poems were first printed: *California Librarian, Cotyledon, Epos, Event, Galley Sail Review, Iconolatre, Invisible City, Mano Mano, The Naked Ear, Notes from Underground, Odyssey, The Outsider, Painted Bride Quarterly, Prairie Schooner, Quagga, Quicksilver, Quixote, Red Tree, Rongwrong, Second Coming, Scream Magazine, The Sparrow, Stonecloud, Sun, Synaesthesia, Targets, Two Charlies, Vagabond, The Wormwood Review.*

Thanks to Mark Gaipa for the good times and the suggestions.

Special thanks to Linda Bukowski for believing in this project from day one.